SPENCER QUINN

D0038465

BOW WOW

A Bowser and Birdie Novel

SCHOLASTIC

ISBN 978-1-338-09136-6

9 781338 091366

50799

BOW WOW

A BOWSER AND BIRDIE NOVEL

SPENCER QUINN

SCHOLASTIC INC.

ISBN 978-1-338-09136-6

10 9 8 7 6 5 4 3 2 1   18 19 20 21 22

Printed in the U.S.A.   40
This edition first printing 2018

The text type was set in Matt Antique.
The display type was set in Gill Sans ® Ultra Bold.
Book design by Kristina Iulo and Elizabeth B. Parisi

TO LILY, WITH THANKS
FOR ALL THE HELP.
—S.Q.

A CAR BEEPED OUTSIDE OUR HOUSE AT 19 Gentilly Lane. *Beep beep.* The *beep beep* of a horn hurts my ears in a way you probably wouldn't understand, since my sense of hearing is a lot different from yours. I didn't say *better* than yours, so don't be upset. But just between you and me, it is better! I hear sounds humans don't hear all the time! For example, that *drip drip drip*, right now, under the kitchen sink? Down in the cupboard with all the cleaning supplies, including some tasty sponges? But never mind the sponges. The point is someone should do something to stop that *drip drip drip*—except they won't because they don't even hear it. There's going to be a big puddly mess, and soon!

The humans in our family all turned to me: Birdie, Mama, Grammy. "What the heck is that blasted barking about?" Grammy said.

Someone was barking? I listened my hardest, heard no barking. This was a strange day already, and it had hardly even started.

"Maybe he's upset you're leaving, Mama," Birdie said.

Mama bent down, gave me a pat. "Is that it, Bowser? Upset that I'm leaving?"

"Bull pucky," said Grammy. "How would he even know you're leaving?"

Whoa! Mistakes were going by so fast I could hardly keep up. Why wouldn't I know Mama was leaving? Wasn't that her suitcase, the sturdy metal kind with straps, all packed and standing by the door, her hard hat perched on top? But that wasn't why I was upset. Not that you could call me upset. I'm known as a pretty steady customer around these parts—these parts being the little bayou town of St. Roch, the nicest little bayou town you'll ever see, and if you happen to be passing through, stop by! And maybe bring a treat, chewies always welcome if nothing else comes to mind. Although here are some hints: steak tips, sausages, hamburger patties. No cooking necessary—I'm not fussy.

But where were we? Something about . . . being upset? Me? Why would I—

Beep beep.

That was it! The beeping! My ears! I was just about to let everyone know how I felt about that beeping in no uncertain terms when Mama said, "Well, kiddo," and wrapped her arms around Birdie, holding her close. "My chariot awaits."

Chariot? That one blew right by me. Maybe here's a chance to describe the family, before we've really gotten going. If not now, how will I ever squeeze it in later? I'll try to be quick. How about we start with Mama? Mama's Birdie's mom, but she's not Grammy's daughter. Grammy's son was Birdie's dad, a police captain who got killed down in New Orleans when Birdie was just little, and not too long ago we found out who did it! And even why! Neither of which I can remember at the moment. Mama's tall and strong, with deep, dark eyes and light brown hair, usually in a ponytail, like now. In these parts we've got some farms and ranches, so you get to know ponies. I love how they use their tails to swish away flies, and I'm sure Mama will figure out how to do that with her own ponytail one day. Mama was an oil platform engineer, which must mean she's pretty smart, and pretty smart means way smarter than any pony, and then some.

Mama's got powerful hands and so does Grammy, even though Grammy's half Mama's size, and kind of old and bony, smelling like stacks of yellowed newspapers down at the town library. Grammy's eyes are washed-out blue and don't miss a thing. Birdie's eyes are also blue, but bright and shining, like the big, blue sky at the nicest time of the nicest day. And is there time to mention Birdie's smell, all about soap and lemons and these lovely yellow flowers that grow on the edge of the bayou, beautiful flowers although not particularly tasty? Probably not—so back to the little front hall at 19 Gentilly Lane, where those deep brown eyes of Mama's seemed kind of damp. "Won't be long, honey," she said.

"Three months," Birdie said. "It used to be two."

"This new company has different rules. But we'll do lots of Skyping."

Birdie nodded. Her eyes seemed to dampen, too. She blinked a few times and gave her head a quick shake, like she was trying to blink and shake that dampness away. Uh-oh. Was Birdie unhappy about something? Not on my watch! I squeezed myself in between them, pressing my head against Birdie to let her know that there was nothing to be unhappy about, not with ol' Bowser in the picture. Birdie's got great balance, so she didn't quite fall down, not all the way to the floor, and the next thing I knew Mama and Birdie were laughing— although not Grammy, who might have been shooting a somewhat severe look my way—and the front door was open.

A car waited in the driveway, a man and a woman in front, luggage on the roof rack. Mama gave Grammy a quick hug.

"Don't work too hard."

"Hrrmf," said Grammy.

Mama picked up her suitcase, kissed the top of Birdie's head. "Love you."

"Love you, too, Mama."

"Take good care of Grammy."

"Ha!" said Grammy.

Mama went out to the car. The trunk popped open. She swung the suitcase inside, got in the backseat. The car drove off. Birdie and Mama waved at each other until it turned the corner and vanished from sight. Then Birdie just stood there, her hand still raised, hanging motionless in the air.

Grammy closed the door and gave Birdie a look. "How about breakfast?"

"I'm not hungry."

"No reason to eat, then." Grammy checked her watch. "Better get ready for school."

"No school today, Grammy. We're on vacation."

"Again? How're you gonna learn anything?"

"I'm getting all As," Birdie said. "With some exceptions." She headed down the hall, me right behind her at first, and then in the lead, which always feels best.

"Where do you think you're going?"

"Back to bed."

"Guess again," said Grammy. "I want you to go open the store."

"But it's not even seven o'clock."

"Time to shake things up." She handed Birdie the keys.

"Shake things up?"

"According to an article in the paper. The secret of doing business in times like these is disruption."

"What's disruption?"

"Shaking things up. I just said. Let's not go around in circles. Life's too short." Then, in a quieter voice, Grammy added, "And hold your head up."

Our store's called Gaux Family Fish and Bait. No way you could miss it, on account of the big sign on the roof in the shape of a fish. We stepped onto the porch, me and Birdie, a long porch crowded with nets and buoys and coils of rope, all smelling swampy. Birdie unlocked the door, took a flyswatter off a wall hook, and started swatting a few flies that had gotten inside overnight. Love flyswatting! Birdie does the actual swatting and I race around the floor, pawing at what's left of the flies when they land.

After that, Birdie dusted off the display cases, full of lures and hooks and knives, and sat on the stool behind the register, gazing at nothing. I sat at her feet and gazed at her.

"Oh, Bowser," she said after a while. "It's not that I don't love Grammy. I do. I love her a whole lot. But . . ."

But what? I had no clue. My only thought was to put my paw on Birdie's knee, so that was what I did. Sometimes it helps to have only one thought, competing thoughts usually upsetting your peace of mind. Me, I'm almost always the one-thought type, just another example of my good luck. Birdie's the luckiest thing that ever happened to me, of course, no need to even mention that, so I won't. Meanwhile, I was enjoying the view through the back window, which looked right out on the bayou, very still the way it gets early in the morning, and at our charter fishing boat, *Bayou Girl*, tied to the dock.

"And what's the point of being here?" Birdie said. "Everyone knows we don't open till eight thirty, so why—"

There may have been more like that, but I got distracted by a pelican that came swooping down from the sky and dove straight into the bayou, the sharp point of its long beak breaking the surface, and then the whole bird disappearing underwater with hardly even a splash. A moment after that, the pelican bobbed up to the surface, a fish now squirming in that beak. Forget it, my fishy friend! I'd seen this many times: The fish never get away, but instead always fall into that enormous pouch of a pelican mouth, and that's that. Which was exactly what happened now, except . . . except what came next was so strange and scary—even though ol' Bowser is scared of nothin'—that I wasn't even sure I actually saw it. Did it really happen? An enormous head, darkish gray-brown in color, burst up from below the surface of the bayou, a fish-type head but way bigger, huge and round like the oil barrels you see on the barges. Or even huger! The size of that wide-open mouth! A sort of lopsided mouth, hard to describe. And those teeth—so many, so big, so sharp! Did I mention thc little eyes, red hot and icy cold at the same time? The pelican—together with the fish still squirming in its beak—got gulped down in a flash.

"Bowser! Bowser! What are you doing?"

What was I doing? I seemed to be standing up, front paws against the glass, possibly barking the tiniest bit.

Birdie rose, came to the window, gazed out. Now there was nothing to see but a ripple or two, plus a single brown feather drifting on the bayou.

"What's gotten into you today?" Birdie said. "Imagine if Grammy . . ."

But I never had to imagine whatever this was, probably not something too good, because the front door opened and a man entered the store. How had he even gotten close without me knowing? Security was my job!

"Hey there," said this man, a small, wiry dude with a deep tan, smelling very fishy.

Birdie straightened up. "Hi," she said.

"Your pooch don't seem to like me a whole lot."

"Bowser! Cool it!"

Cool it? Cool what? Had some sort of growling started up inside Gaux Family Fish and Bait? That was annoying. If there was any growling to be done, that was the department of yours truly, ol' Bowser, and nobody but nobody—

"Bowser!"

I got a grip.

The dude glanced around the store. He was dressed like a lot of dudes we see—baggy shorts, faded T, dirty sneaks—and had long, stringy hair and bandy legs. Also, he had that squinty-eyed look that comes from lots of time on the water under the sun's glare. "Fella name of Snoozy LaChance work here?" he said.

"Yes," said Birdie.

"When's he expected?"

Even I knew that was a tough question. There's no telling with Snoozy. Snoozy's our assistant at the shop, but he kind of comes and goes. What can I tell you about Snoozy? The second-most interesting thing about him is how quickly he can fall asleep, even quicker than me. The most interesting thing? His tattoos. Snoozy has tattoos of different kinds of fish all over both arms. When he flexes his muscles it's like the fish are swimming around, except he hardly has any muscles, so the fish don't move much.

"Um," Birdie said. "Later."

"How much later?"

"I'm not sure."

"Not sure? Heck of a way to run a business."

I'm the type who likes humans, pretty much each and every one I've ever met—except for one or two who didn't treat Birdie right, and I'm sure they'll recover from their wounds very soon, except for two real bad guys, one taken care of by a gator and the other by a cottonmouth. But . . . but . . . where was I going with this? Oh, right, the wiry dude: I was starting not to like him. At the moment, he was glancing around the store.

"Who's in charge here?" he said.

"Me," said Birdie.

"You? You're a kid."

The wiry dude got that right. Birdie was a kid—eleven years old, as I well knew because I was her birthday present—and the greatest possible kid in all of bayou country, although I didn't like the way he said it. I eased my way over in his direction. He had skinny calf muscles, hardly worth sinking your teeth into, but if security's your job, you can't be a prima donna. I hope "prima donna" fits here—it's a favorite expression of Grammy's. She also likes "dumber than a post" and "don't bring a spoon to a fork fight," both a complete mystery to me.

"When he shows up," the wiry dude said, digging into his back pocket, "tell him to get in touch with me. Pronto." He laid a card on the counter in front of Birdie, a very unfresh-looking card that smelled of gasoline and bait worms. And whoa! It wasn't just the card: The dude himself smelled of gasoline and bait worms.

He turned and walked out of the store. Most flip-floppers make a *slap-slap* sound when they walk, but this dude had a silent walk, silent for a human. I filed that fact away, tried to remember what it was, and almost succeeded! Wow!

Birdie peered at the card without picking it up. "'Captain Deke Waylon,'" she read. "'Best sport fishing on the Gulf Coast. Hook 'em every time or the day is free!'" Birdie glanced my way. "Or the day is free? How's that possible?" She leaned forward, gazed closer at the card. "Wait a minute—here's an asterisk." She flipped the card over, held it to the light, then took a magnifying glass from a drawer and examined it again. "'Tiniest writing I've ever seen, Bowser. I think it says 'Additional charges apply.'"

Not long after that, Junior Tebbets came into the store. Junior's a real skinny kid with a Mohawk haircut and an earring in one ear. He's a pal of Birdie's, and, therefore, of mine, too—better believe it!—and so are Nola, whose

11

family owns the general store, and Rory, whose dad is the sheriff. Junior's dad, Wally, runs the food truck that's usually parked on our side of the Lucinda Street Bridge, the nearest bayou crossing, and lots of times—like now!—Junior shows up with some spare food. What else do you need to know about Junior? For one thing, he's into music—the drums particularly—and I've heard his distant drumming a few times late at night, but Rory said someone called his dad about it and now there's no more nighttime drumming.

"Hey," he said.

"Hi, Junior."

"You're in early today."

"Yeah."

"How come?"

Birdie shrugged her shoulders.

"Hungry?" Junior said.

"No."

"I brought you a po'boy. Shrimp and red pepper, the kind you like."

"No, thanks."

"I've only taken a couple of little bites."

"I'm not hungry."

"You're kind of prickly today, Birdie."

"Prickly?"

"That's what my stepmom always called my dad—prickly. Not talkin' about my stepmom now, or the one before, but the one before that. It means—"

"I know what prickly means."

"Okeydokey, artichokey."

"Okeydokey artichokey?"

"That's what my new stepmom says when she's in a good mood, meaning hardly ever."

Birdie gave Junior not the friendliest sort of look.

"What about Bowser?" Junior said.

"What about him?"

"Any chance he's hungry?"

Birdie shook her head. "He already had a big bowl of kibble."

Whoa! Not so fast! Big bowl of kibble? When was that, exactly? I'd certainly had bowls of kibble in my life—none I would really call big, by the way—but they were all faint memories.

"Bowser! Don't beg."

"What makes you think he's begging?"

"Junior! He's sitting on your feet! His mouth's wide open! That's begging!"

"He is drooling a bit," Junior said.

Oh, no! Drooling? Me? That didn't sound like the way to go. But how can you stop drooling? I got very confused, and in my confusion might have snatched that po'boy with shrimp and red peppers right out of Junior's hand and taken care of it in one bite. All I knew for sure was that the po'boy seemed to have vanished and there may have been a shrimpy taste in my mouth.

Oh, and one more thing: Birdie and Junior were staring at me, their eyes wide open. I got the feeling I might be in some sort of trouble, but then came a lovely surprise. Birdie tilted back her head and started laughing. She has the loveliest laugh in the world. She laughed and laughed, and I ran crazily around the store, and then Junior was laughing, too. At the end, Birdie's laughter turned to tears a bit, which she brushed away with the back of her hand, giving her head a quick little shake.

"Whew," said Junior. "Back to normal. Maybe now we can talk business." He took a thick sheet of paper from his pocket, unfolded it, and handed it to Birdie.

Birdie looked it over. "A song?" she said. "What's all this?"

"Song contest, sponsored by WSBY, the Voice of Bayou Country. All entries must be original songs, and the winner gets five thousand dollars and a free trip to Nashville that includes a meeting with a genuine record producer. Plus a year's supply of cleaning products from Kroger's."

"What kind of cleaning products?"

"I'm not sure. But the point is there's a deadline for

entries." Junior jabbed at the paper. "We've got three weeks to write and record an original song."

"Who is we?"

"Me on drums, Nola on guitar, you on vocals."

"Forget it."

"Just like that? You've got a great voice, Birdie. Everyone says so."

"Name one actual person."

"Mr. Savoy."

"The librarian?"

"He says you've got music in your blood."

Uh-oh. I'd tasted human blood on a number of occasions, some of them pretty action packed, but did not recall any music in the mix.

"He's talking about Grammy's father," Birdie said. "Mr. Savoy found a record he made. But that doesn't mean—"

"Sure it does! Ever heard of Bach?"

"No."

"Me neither. But Mr. Savoy says music ran in his family for, like, centuries. And then there's your name—Birdie. Think that happened for no reason?"

"It happened because it's a good southern name, and my parents couldn't agree on anything else."

"Got to be more to it than that. The word *fate* mean anything to you?"

"It's my fate to be in a band with you and Nola?"

"You got it!"

Birdie gave Junior a long look. For a moment, she reminded me of Grammy! How was that possible? A weird and frightening thought—I got rid of it at my very fastest. "Tell you what," Birdie said. "I'm in if Nola's in—which, by the way, will be never."

"Wrong on that one," said Junior. "She already said yes."

"What?"

"The lure of fame is strong, my friend," Junior said. He handed Birdie a pencil on his way out of the store. "I think we should aim for a written song by lunchtime."

2

OT LONG AFTER THAT, GRAMMY APPEARED.

"Any customers?"

"Not yet, Grammy. But it's early."

"Hrrmf."

"But someone came by looking for Snoozy." She handed Grammy the card that the little wiry dude—Captain Deke Waylon—had given her.

Grammy peered at it. "Waylon?" she said. "Would that be one of those good-for-nothing Waylons from down in Baie LaRouche?"

"I don't know, Grammy. How come they're good for nothing?"

"Corner cutters, each and every one, going way back."

"What are corner cutters?"

I was interested in the answer myself—corner cutting sounded like something speedy and fun—but Grammy had no time to explain, because the door opened and another person came in. All sorts of foot traffic this morning, although we didn't seem to be doing any actual business, actual business meaning money passing from the customers' hands to ours. Not mine personally, of course, although I've snapped up money in my mouth on more than one occasion. Always a thrill! Then comes the opposite of a thrill, when Grammy catches sight of what's going on.

But back to this new person, who turned out to be Sheriff Cannon, father of our pal Rory, which I might have mentioned already. The sheriff's got the sort of face that's hard to ignore, with a square chin, big nose, and bushy eyebrows. Also he's tall and strong, and folks often back away a step or two when he's around. Not Grammy. She backs away from nobody.

"Hi, there, Miz Gaux," he said. "And Birdie."

"Hi," said Birdie.

"Sheriff," said Grammy.

Sheriff Cannon looked down at Birdie. "Rory says hi."

"Hi back," Birdie said.

This conversation, although short so far, was not easy to follow.

"We're having a cookout week from Sunday," the sheriff said. "He wondered if you'd like to drop by."

"Uh, thanks," Birdie said.

"And bring Bowser along—I'm guessing he's a fan of cookouts."

Wow! The sheriff turned out to be a great guesser! I'd

always been a little wary of the sheriff, but now I gave some serious consideration to going over to him and sitting on his foot, possibly even licking his hand.

Meanwhile, Grammy was looking impatient. "You came here to invite Birdie to a cookout?"

"No, ma'am," the sheriff said, and he was the one who took a step back. "I'm actually looking for help with an investigation."

"What kind of investigation?"

"Well, maybe it's too soon to call it an investigation. What I need is your advice, as someone who knows our local waters better than anybody."

"Not so sure about that," Grammy said.

"Oh, Grammy," said Birdie. "Who knows better than you?"

Grammy shot her a sharp glance, Grammy language for *zip it, partner*. Birdie zipped it. "Go on, Sheriff," she said.

"You familiar with bull sharks?" he said.

"Pah," said Grammy.

"Meaning you are?" the sheriff said. "Or you don't like them? Or what?"

"Who likes a bull shark?" Grammy said. "Have to be out of your mind."

"Is there anything particularly unlikable about them? Compared to other sharks?"

"That's a big subject," Grammy said. "Let's just put it this way: Bulls are big, aggressive, hang out close to shore, and don't scare easy, suppose you wanted to shoo them away."

"Shoo them away?" said the sheriff. "I don't understand."

"Ever done any spearfishing?" Grammy said.

"No."

"Well, that's what I'm talking about. Say you're snorkeling out in the Gulf, and you just speared a nice red snapper, and all of a sudden, out of the gloom, comes a big bull shark who wants to take it away from you. Can't let that happen, so you gotta shoo that shark away—except it's hard to get them to cooperate, like I said."

Birdie's eyes opened wide. "Were you a diver, Grammy?"

"Not a scuba tank diver," said Grammy. "What's the sport in that? We were free divers."

"Who's 'we,' Grammy?"

"Me and my friends."

"Do I know any of them?"

Grammy shook her head. "All gone now."

"Drowned?"

"Drowned? Where'd you get an idea like that?"

"I just thought—"

"Whoa," said the sheriff. "Can we back up a bit? This was all free diving?"

"Didn't I just explain that?" Grammy said.

"What's free diving?" said Birdie.

"When you hold your breath," the sheriff told her. He turned to Grammy. "How deep did you go?"

"Not much compared to what they're doing nowadays. Seventy, eighty feet or so."

"Grammy!"

"And way down there a bull shark would sometimes try to take a fish off your spear?" the sheriff said.

"Didn't I just explain that?" Grammy said again.

The sheriff nodded. "So I take it you must have shooed away some bull sharks successfully."

"Successfully? Where'd you get that idea?"

"You're still here," the sheriff said.

"But those darned sharks stole my fish every single time! Right off the spear! Sometimes they even tried to take my gun—can you imagine?"

"How did you stop them?"

"Bopped them on the snout, of course. How else do you shoo off a shark?"

"Bopped them with what?" the sheriff said.

"Why, the end of the spear gun barrel. Maybe my fist, once or twice."

"You—you punched a shark with your fist, Grammy?"

"I was ticked," said Grammy. "Most sharks, you bop

them on the snout, they swim off. Not used to it, you see. Their normal prey just turns and tries to hightail it— exactly the wrong move. But your bull shark maybe backs off for a bit, and then sometimes comes in again. Which used to tick me off even more!"

"So they're more persistent than other sharks?" said the sheriff.

"Didn't I just explain?"

What? Grammy was saying that again? I got the idea this conversation wasn't going well. As for bull sharks, I was a little fuzzy on what they were. Something like gators? I'd had a run-in with a gator once, had no desire to do it again. Then a thought came right up to the edge of my mind, a thought about pelicans. I got the feeling this was going to be an important thought but just like that—*zip!*— it vanished. Did I fret about that? Not for a second! That wouldn't have been me.

Meanwhile, the sheriff was starting to look a little ticked himself. "I'm just trying to get up to speed, Miz Gaux, if you'll be patient."

Grammy crossed her arms over her chest. "Why?"

"I'm coming to that," the sheriff said. "First, is it true that bull sharks can survive in freshwater?"

Grammy nodded.

"How can they do that, Grammy?" Birdie said.

"Kidneys," said Grammy. "They got special kidneys."

"So finding bull sharks up rivers and bayous wouldn't be surprising," the sheriff said.

"Can't say I'd put it like that," said Grammy. "A bit of a shock to most folks, especially if they're swimming at the time."

"How far up rivers and bayous?" the sheriff said. "Like, in terms of our own bayou, for example."

"Don't know for sure," said Grammy. "Five, ten miles from the ocean, maybe."

"How about as far as Betencourt Bridge?"

"Betencourt Bridge?" Grammy said. "That's seven miles farther on up the bayou from us, and we're thirty-three miles from the sea. There's never been a bull shark in St. Roch, not as long as I've been here."

"But how can you be sure?" the sheriff said, adding "ma'am" when he caught the look crossing Grammy's face.

"You asked my opinion," Grammy said. "I answered."

"Right," the sheriff said. "But supposing a bull shark went by undetected. At night, say, underwater, and when you were asleep."

Grammy asleep? It did happen, but she was a very light sleeper, as I'd learned late one night when I'd caught a whiff of pizza left on the kitchen counter and set off silently down the hall. I'd relearned the same lesson several times after that—once with a burger and once with pizza, again. The point being: Nothing got past Grammy.

The sheriff gazed down at her. Grammy gazed up at him. Some humans radiate a kind of force you can feel. The sheriff and Grammy were two of a kind that way, Grammy even more so.

"How about doing me a favor?" the sheriff said at last.

"Like what?" said Grammy.

"I've got a citizen up in Betencourt Bridge who claims he had an encounter with a bull shark Thursday evening. Actually, the encounter was with his twelve-year-old son. They're pretty upset—the dad went out on his boat blasting away with a twelve-gauge at what turned out to be shadows in the bayou, plus a catfish. I'd like you to come up there and help out, as a kind of expert witness."

"Was the son hurt?" Birdie said.

"No physical damage," the sheriff said. "But he got a pretty good scare thrown into him, and lost his rod and reel."

Then came a silence where Grammy seemed to be thinking and Birdie and the sheriff seemed to be watching her think.

"Why not?" Birdie said. "Let's do it, Grammy."

"Oh?" said Grammy. "And who's going to mind the store?"

Which was the moment the front door opened once

again and Snoozy walked in. When were we going to get an actual paying customer?

"Hey, everybody!" Snoozy said. Snoozy had on his usual outfit—sleeveless T-shirt, shorts with sagging cargo pockets, red flip-flops—and wore two pairs of sunglasses, one perched on his head, the other dangling on a Croakie around his neck. Snoozy had a large Croakie collection. This one was decorated with tiny mermaids. "What's the occasion?"

"Snoozy can watch the store," Birdie said.

"Yeah, sure," said Snoozy. "Especially since that's why I'm here!" And he started laughing like something funny had just happened. Snoozy was one of those people who shake when they laugh, meaning all his fish tattoos shook, too.

No one else was laughing. "That's exactly why you're here, but not for much longer," Grammy said.

"Huh?" said Snoozy.

"Do you realize you're half an hour late?"

Snoozy cast an alarmed glance at his wristwatch, only to find he wasn't wearing one. But there was a blue crab tattoo on his wrist, which distracted him for a moment.

Grammy's voice sharpened. "Snoozy!"

"Uh, sorry," he said. "I'll come in—what did you say? Half an hour? I'll come in half an hour early next time, balance everything out nicely."

Grammy gave him a look I wouldn't want to get. She turned to the sheriff. "Okay," she said. "I'll do it."

We headed for the door, with me nosing ahead of Sheriff Cannon just as we went through, the sheriff grunting, but not necessarily in pain: I'd hardly brushed his knee. What's important is that I got out first, as I'm sure the sheriff would tell you when he's in a good mood. Getting through doorways first is part of my job, although it's hard to explain why.

"Hey! Where's the party?" Snoozy said.

Grammy handed him Deke Waylon's card on our way out.

"What's this?" Snoozy said.

By that time we were in the parking lot, the door closing firmly behind us.

"This, uh, gentleman up in Betencourt Bridge is new to the parish," the sheriff said we drove onto the highway.

We were all in his cruiser—Grammy up front in the shotgun seat, my favorite spot in any vehicle, although I was cool with the setup this time, on account of having Birdie beside me in the back.

"Hails from up north," the sheriff went on. "Chicago, or maybe Milwaukee."

"Uh-huh," said Grammy, not sounding interested. I was with her on that. Where were we going? Why? I had no idea. But car rides were always fun. Sometimes, for example, you came upon a car with a cat lying on the shelf by the rear window! And then you barked your head off at that stuck-up little critter! Makes your whole day, every time. I sat up straighter.

"What's he doing here, this guy from up north?" Birdie said.

"Important question," said the sheriff. "Mr. Kronik is building call centers."

"What are those?" Birdie said.

The sheriff glanced at her in the rearview mirror. "Like when you call because your computer's frozen, or your remote's gotten screwy, or there's a mistake in a credit card bill. That voice on the other end is coming from a call center."

"Call centers in Betencourt Bridge?" Grammy said.

"Cheapest land in the parish," said the sheriff.

"And cheapest labor, too," said Grammy.

"I don't know the stats on that."

"Don't need stats. Just look around at how folks live."

I looked around, saw cane fields on one side, the bayou on the other, and in the distance flares rising from a gas well, fiery orange against the big blue sky. No actual folks around except for us, and we seemed to be living just fine. What more could we want? A cat to bark at?

Grammy twisted around in my direction. "What in heck's he barkin' about?"

"Bowser," Birdie said, putting her hand on my back.

Barking? That was me? I was barking at . . . at nothing. So maybe there was no good reason. I got a grip in no time flat, went so silent you wouldn't have known I was there.

We drove into a town, smaller than St. Roch, not as nicely kept up, and even the bayou wasn't as blue. "Betencourt Bridge," the sheriff said.

"Where's the bridge?" said Birdie.

"Got blown up in the Civil War," said the sheriff.

"A long time ago," Birdie said.

"Hrrmf," said Grammy.

The sheriff followed a road beside the bayou, which soon widened into a big lake with yellow earthmovers crawling around a big construction site at one end and a marina at the other. We parked at the marina and walked down to the dock, where a very big houseboat was tied up.

"Mostly house, not much boat" was something Grammy often said about houseboats, and this one—so tall and wide—was like that and even more so. A man was pacing back and forth on the top deck, a cell phone at each ear. Sheriff Cannon waved to him. The man ignored him, kept pacing and talking, sounding pretty angry on one phone and really angry on the other. He disappeared behind the wheelhouse, and when he reappeared both phone conversations were over, the phones clipped to his belt. He looked down at us.

"Gannon?" he said.

"Cannon," said the sheriff. "Sheriff Cannon."

"Uh-huh," said the man. "And what?"

He was short and very thick, his neck especially, and wore one of those neatly trimmed beards you don't see much around these parts, most of our bearded dudes sporting the unruly type. I prefer unruly beards on account of how food morsels can get caught in them and sometimes, if you're lucky, fall to the floor. Unless you catch them in midair, of course—one of my specialties.

"And what?" said the sheriff.

"I mean," the man said, "how come you're back here?"

"Just following up on our talk."

"What for? We told you the whole story. Meanwhile, that killer is out there waiting for his next victim." He made a jabbing motion toward the water.

"Not sure there's been a victim yet," the sheriff said.

"Am I hearing right? Have you forgotten Holden?"

"Well, he wasn't actually hurt."

"Not hurt? The kid was traumatized!"

"I meant physically," the sheriff said. The man started sputtering something, but the sheriff talked over him.

"What I'd like to do first is gather some more information. I've brought an expert on our local waters. Mr. Miles Kronik, meet Miz Claire Gaux."

"How do," said Grammy.

Mr. Miles Kronik glanced down at Grammy and said nothing.

"Can we come aboard?" said the sheriff.

That was when Kronik noticed me for the first time. "Is that a dog?" he said.

Wow! I'd already gotten the idea that this dude was from somewhere else, but somewhere else without dogs? Like he was seeing one for the first time? What a shocker! Who'd even want to live there, a dogless place? Not me, buster. And of course I . . . I actually couldn't. At that point I got confused and might have lost the thread.

Around then was when Birdie spoke up. "His name is Bowser," she said.

All my confusion went away. You had to love Birdie, and I do.

3

BOWSER, SCHMOWSER, WHATEVER," MR. Kronik said. "No dogs on board."

And just like that, I was right back smack-dab in confusion. Schmowser? There was a dog named Schmowser suddenly in the picture? I saw no dog, and neither did I smell one, which should have done it for me. No dog, case closed. But the thought of a new buddy is always exciting, as I'm sure you know. And don't forget the smack-dab-in-confusion part. Combine confusion and excitement and what do you get? In this case: Bowser in midair.

Yes, me in midair, off the dock, across a narrow strip of water, and onto the lower deck of the houseboat, sticking that landing perfectly, with not a wobble and hardly even a sound. Although there were sounds to be heard—don't get me wrong about that! Those sounds were human sounds, a rising hubbub of confusion and excitement. Confusion and excitement? Wow! As though the state of my own mind was spreading to others! Like my mind was taking over the whole world! My mind had never done anything like that in the past, not even close. I felt so full of joy I can't even tell you, like I could take off and fly, which is sort of what I did, charging down the deck of the houseboat, paws hardly touching down, hell-bent in pursuit of . . . of . . . of Schmowser, that was it! Almost forgot! Hell-bent in pursuit of Schmowser, my new best pal. And what a pal he was going to be, unseeable, unsmellable. The fun we were going to—

OOMPH!

Oomph? Maybe I haven't described where I was very well, but, in truth, I hardly knew myself. The main thing was that I was running along the deck, a stretch of deck at the bow, with handrails on one side and the wall of the house on the other, a wall with windows and flowerpots on sills, and doors. Doors were the important part because with no warning one of those doors opened and out stepped a boy, squarish and thick-necked, busy with something on his phone, his stubby nose practically touching the screen.

Now, back to oomph. OOMPH! I barreled into this squarish boy full speed, an enormous collision that sent the two of us flying—me actually upside down for a bit, my face to the sky, an interesting sensation—up, up, and over the top bow rail, clearing it by plenty, followed by a long, slow fall, down and down and into the lake, *splash*, *splash*.

I hadn't actually planned on a swim, but swimming is something I love—and am very good at, even though I never had one single lesson. So when I bobbed up to the surface, I started paddling around a bit, using the dog paddle, one of the greatest inventions of me and my kind. I was trying to think of another when I became aware of a big commotion going on.

On the top deck of the houseboat, Mr. Kronik was jumping up and down and screaming, "He can't swim! He can't swim!"

Which was crazy! I'm a natural-born swimmer, as I was demonstrating at that very moment. Meanwhile, on the dock, the sheriff was handing Grammy his gun belt and Birdie was shouting, "Bowser! Bowser!" Not sure why, but there was no time to figure it out, because the kid—hair now plastered over his head and his phone still clutched in one hand, which struck me as kind of odd—came bursting to the surface, sputtering and gasping.

"Holden can't swim! He can't swim!"

I got the picture! It was this kid who couldn't swim, not me. All the kids I knew—Birdie, Nola, Junior, Rory, and lots of others—were good swimmers, but if this kid was not, then there was nothing to do but edge up against him, keep his head up and out of the water, and herd him over to the dock. I edged up immediately, and that was when

the kid noticed me, his eyes opening wide in fear—
and they were already opened wide in fear to begin with,
so this was fear to the max.

Was this kid the son of Mr. Kronik? He kind of looked
like him, and he certainly screamed like him.

"A dog! A dog!"

No arguing with that. I was as doggy as they come, and
proud of it. I got myself positioned nicely against the kid's
shoulder. Our eyes met, mine sending a message that
everything was cool, and his . . . well, his were sending
some other sort of message.

"Arrrgh! Arrrgh! A dog!"

Up on the top deck, Mr. Kronik was still jumping up
and down. "He's petrified of dogs! He's petrified of dogs!"

Petrified meaning what exactly? Good or bad? No
chance to find out, because Holden—if I'd caught his
name—had started thrashing around. Thrash, thrash,
thrash, and then he sank suddenly from sight.

"Sheriff!" shrieked Mr. Kronik. "Don't just stand there,
you moron! I can't swim, either!"

Mr. Kronik couldn't swim, either? But Sheriff Cannon
was the moron? I tried to make sense of that as I dove
down, grabbed Holden by the collar, and hauled him up to
the surface. Was he pleased about that? Sputter, sputter,
and then, "A dog! A dog!" Around that point was when the

sheriff came swimming up. We steered Holden over to the dock, the sheriff and I. Birdie and Grammy pulled the kid out of the water. The sheriff scrambled out on his own, and so did I.

One funny thing. Just as I was almost on the dock, half on it and half of me still in the water, I felt something brushing past my tail. Just a light touch, hardly there at all, but somehow it sent a big and mighty message. I hopped onto the dock, gave myself a long and very energetic shake, the kind that usually gets humans laughing. And maybe some humans somewhere were laughing, but not any of the humans in my vicinity, not even Birdie.

"Now, Holden," said the sheriff, dressed in civilian clothes he'd had in the trunk of the cruiser, "I'd appreciate it if you'd tell Miz Gaux here the whole story in your own words."

"Who else's would I use?" said the kid, wrapped in a towel and sitting in a nice sort of living room at the stern of the houseboat. Stern is boating lingo for the back: You learn stuff like that living in bayou country.

Meanwhile, had this kid, Holden if I was following things right, just sent some sort of smart-ass remark the sheriff's way? From the expressions on the faces of the sheriff and Grammy, I would have thought so, but Mr. Kronik seemed to be smiling in a proud-dad sort of way. Kind of confusing. Whoa! Confused again, and so soon? I considered another round of sprinting and possibly even swimming. No way, of course, not in my immediate future, first because I was on the leash, highly unusual in an indoor situation, and second because Birdie—sitting right beside me on a chair in this living room at the end farthest from all the others—had told me I was in the doghouse. I used to get excited at that thought: a house of my own! Treats galore! But it turned out that every mention of a doghouse was followed by an unpleasant period—like being on the leash indoors, for example, or not being included on an outing with Birdie and her friends. And the truth was I didn't really want a house of my own. I preferred things the way they were, living forever with Birdie at 19 Gentilly Lane.

Meanwhile, the sheriff was saying, ". . . so you went fishing in the bayou?"

"Yeah," said Holden. "I rowed out in the dinghy."

"Out where?" said the sheriff.

"Into this lake or whatever it is," Holden said. "Then I dropped the thingy in and waited."

"Thingy?" said the sheriff.

"You know—to attract the fish."

"Lure," said the sheriff.

"Whatever," Holden said.

Grammy folded her hands. "Done much fishing?"

Holden shook his head. "That was my first time." Then came a silence, and he added, "But it's not rocket science."

Whatever that was about, Grammy and the sheriff didn't like it. Their faces—so different—made the exact same frown. How interesting was that? And then I happened to take in the expression on Birdie's face, and she was also doing the exact same frown! This little get-together must have been going badly, but I didn't know why.

"So," said the sheriff, "you're waiting with the thingy in the water."

"Yeah," Holden said. "Bo-ring. Then the mosquitoes came and all these other pests you've got down here, and I was just thinking of bagging the whole thing when it happened."

"When what happened?" the sheriff said.

"When the bull shark attacked me. Isn't that what we're talking about?"

The sheriff gave Holden a look you couldn't call friendly. "Describe this attack."

"Excuse me," said Mr. Kronik. "You're saying attack in quotes—like you don't believe my son."

"Oh?" the sheriff said. "Must be our local accent down here."

"No problem with the accent," said Mr. Kronik.

"Customers calling in are going to love it—down-home, unthreatening. That's what our research tells us." Mr. Kronik looked down his nose at the sheriff. A stubby nose, maybe not ideal for the full looking-down effect, but Mr. Kronik made the best of it. "No need to remind you that we'll be creating two hundred and fifty jobs, minimum."

The sheriff started to say something but stopped himself. Grammy nodded, like she was agreeing with what he hadn't said. Humans could be so complicated! And then she herself spoke. "No need."

Mr. Kronik shot her a narrow-eyed look. Grammy raised her eyebrows at him, maybe meaning, *Go on—let's hear it.* Hey! Were Grammy and Mr. Kronik about to throw down? My money—of which I have none—was on Grammy.

Nothing like that happened, maybe because Holden brought things back to him.

"Hey! Do you wanna hear or not?"

"I do, for one," Grammy said.

Holden turned to her. "So I was jiggling the lure thingy and all of a sudden this huge head comes blasting up out of the water. Like . . . like a monster. Just that head was longer than the whole dinghy. And the mouth—wide open! Teeth like this, maybe bigger." Holden held his hands far apart. "And then—chomp!—it snapped up my rod and dove down out of sight."

"You must have been scared," the sheriff said.

"Hello?" said Holden. "Almost getting eaten alive?"

"Terrible thing," the sheriff said. "What happened after that?"

"I rowed right back here and told my dad."

Mr. Kronik nodded. "Then we matched Holden's description to our *Fish of the Gulf of Mexico Field Guide*."

"Bull shark," Holden said. "For sure. They can live in freshwater, as you may or may not know."

"And your particular bull shark was kind of special, wasn't it, Holden?"

Holden nodded.

"Special?" said the sheriff.

"It had a scar on one side of its mouth," Holden said. "Like it was always grinning this lopsided grin."

"Lopsided grin," said Mr. Kronik. "The boy's own description."

Did I hear Grammy utter a very soft "Pah!" at that moment? I wasn't sure; no one else could have possibly heard it.

The sheriff turned to Grammy. "Any questions, Miz Gaux?"

"What brand was the rod-and-reel combo?" Grammy said.

Holden shrugged.

"Orvis," said Mr. Kronik. "I ordered it from the Orvis catalog."

"How much?"

"Nine hundred bucks. On sale."

"Whoa," said Birdie, very softly.

Grammy took a notebook and a pencil from her pocket.

"What are you doing?" said Mr. Kronik.

"Making a sketch."

Grammy could make sketches, whatever they were? This was new.

"Sketch of what, Grammy?" Birdie said.

Why didn't we simply amble over there and see? Birdie's hand tightened on the leash. A puzzling moment. Before I could sort things out, Grammy came to us and held up the sketch.

"That's so good," Birdie said.

I eyed the sketch. A big fish of some sort. And all at once, it came back to me! The pelican! And what had happened to it. At first, I thought this was the same kind of fish, but it was thinner and the mouth was not nearly so wide, plus the head was more snakish than bullish. What was going on? I was lost.

Grammy took the sketch over to Holden. One glance was all he needed. "Yup. That's it."

"Sure?" Grammy said. "Don't be hasty."

"No doubt about it."

"Much obliged," said Grammy. She turned to Mr. Kronik. "An easy mistake to make, especially for a newcomer."

"Huh?"

"This here's a member of the gar family, a primitive species we've got down here. Purely a freshwater species, I should point out. This particular kind is called the alligator gar. Not any kind of gator, you understand—just the biggest of the gars."

"Huh?" said Holden again.

One thing I knew: The human who got another human to say "huh" over and over was the one who was winning.

"Wait a minute here," Mr. Kronik said. "You're trying to tell me that Holden saw a gar or whatever the heck this is? Not a bull shark?"

"If the child saw anything at all," Grammy said.

"What is that supposed to mean?"

"No way any bull shark would come this far up the bayou—have to get past at least two shallows on the way, depending on the time of year. And losing such an expensive rig would be upsetting to anybody, regardless of age."

Silence fell in this fancy-pants living room on board Mr. Kronik's fancy-pants houseboat. One other change was the color of Mr. Kronik's face, which went purple.

"Are you calling my son a liar?"

"I'm no name caller, sir."

Mr. Kronik glared at Grammy. He was still glaring at her when he spoke to the sheriff, a strange moment, from where I sat.

"This is just what everybody warned me about before I came down here—all your second-rate, backwater ways. So, not unexpected, and in fact, I'm already working around you."

"Working around me?" the sheriff said, his face on its own way to purple.

"Since you won't do your duty and hunt down the killer bull shark," Mr. Kronik said, turning toward the sheriff in a slow but aggressive way. "Yesterday I put out a bounty on that monster—fifty grand to whoever brings in the body, no questions asked."

"Fifty grand?" said the sheriff.

"We'll get some good publicity out of it," said Mr. Kronik. "And my accountants assure me the expense is tax deductible—looking out for worker safety. So it's a win-win, Sheriff. I'll let you show yourselves out."

He looked down his nose at the sheriff again, but now with the sheriff—a much taller man—on his feet, he didn't get much mileage out of it.

"Not sure I fully understand your take, Miz Gaux," the sheriff said as we drove back to St. Roch.

"It's a fish story," Grammy said. "I've heard 'em all."

"Meaning that snot-nosed little—meaning the kid saw an alligator gar? Or nothing at all?"

"Nothing at all, most likely. He lost his rig somehow—probably just careless—and made up the whole story so's his daddy wouldn't tan his hide."

We drove on for a bit and then Birdie spoke. "Grammy? I'm not sure they're the kind of family that goes in for that."

"In for what?"

"Tanning kids' hides."

"Well, neither are we, now that you mention it. I just meant it as an expression for some kind of strict punishment. We're talking about a nine-hundred-dollar rig!"

We drove on a bit more and Birdie spoke again. "I'm not sure they're the kind of family where nine hundred dollars matter."

Grammy didn't say anything to that, just sat up front, very still.

After a while, the sheriff spoke up. "Two hundred and fifty jobs. And now I'll have bounty hunters all over the bayou."

"When are you up for reelection?" Grammy said.

"Next spring, and I hope I have your support."

"Won't help you much," said Grammy.

Back in St. Roch, the sheriff dropped us off at Gaux Family Fish and Bait. We walked up to the door. The red sign was up, meaning we were closed. Grammy unlocked the door. No one inside, that no one including Snoozy.

"What in the name of—" Grammy began, and then her hand went to her chest and she sagged against a stacked-up display of hibachis. Most humans would have knocked all those hibachis right over, but most humans were a lot bigger than Grammy. The hibachis didn't budge.

4

GRAMMY?" BIRDIE SAID, RUSHING OVER TO her and taking her arm. "Are you okay?"

For a moment, Grammy seemed to lean her weight on Birdie. She said something that was soft and croaky, then licked her lips and tried again. "I'm . . . just fine. Need a moment, that's all."

"Sure, Grammy. How about sitting down?" Birdie reached back with one foot, hooked the leg of a nearby stool, and slid it closer. What a cool move, and without even looking! There's no one like Birdie.

She got Grammy seated on the stool, fetched her a glass of water, tilted it up to Grammy's mouth. Grammy drank. Color came back to her face, which had gone all pasty and gray.

"That's better," she said. "Thank you, Birdie."

"Oh, good," said Birdie. "But what happened?"

Grammy took in a breath. It made a slight wheezing sound. "Nothing to speak of." Grammy held the glass on her own, drank more water. "I'll be back to normal in a flash."

"Oh, good," Birdie said again. "But Grammy? Have you been taking your pills?"

Grammy's voice changed, got much closer to its normal don't-mess-with-me self. "What a question! Why wouldn't I?"

"I don't know," Birdie said. "But Dr. Rajatawan says it's important for you to take all your pills and at the right times and in the right order."

"Easy for him to say."

"Mama thinks he's the best doctor we've ever had in St. Roch."

"Annoying busybody!"

Birdie's eyebrows—so beautifully shaped, the prettiest eyebrows you'd ever want to see—rose up. "Mama?"

"Of course not Mama! Mama's no busybody—she's one of us. I meant Dr. Rajatawan. In fact, I just decided this very moment to get myself one of those second opinions."

"From who, Grammy?"

"Mrs. Roux, down at Roux's Drugs."

"But Mrs. Roux's not a doctor," Birdie said. "She's not even a pharmacist. She just runs the gift shop at the front."

"Don't be snotty," Grammy said. "Like those horrible Kroniks. Is that what the world's coming to?"

"They weren't that bad," Birdie said. "And the whole visit was kind of fun in a way."

And then, all of a sudden, they were both looking at me. Why? I had no idea. And as if that wasn't enough of a surprise, the next thing I knew they were both laughing. Here's something very strange you might not have guessed: Grammy's laugh sounds like the laugh of a young person—actually, almost identical to Birdie's. As for what was funny, you tell me.

No idea how long this laughfest might have lasted, but the door opened. Snoozy? No. A paying customer at last? Not that, either. Instead, this was Snoozy's uncle, Lem LaChance, who sometimes dropped in to sell us crabs or crawfish but never bought anything. He was a pretty big dude, but of the lumpy sort, and rocked a long, grayish ponytail. Grammy called him a one-man revenue stream for every bar in town, so he must have been spending money somewhere, just not here. I couldn't take it further than that.

"Hi, y'all," he said. "Miz Gaux. Birdie. And the best-lookin' pooch in the whole stinkin' swamp."

Did I mention what a fine man Uncle Lem was? Forget all that other stuff about him.

Grammy rose, a little unsteady, but only for a moment. "Just the man I want to see."

"Really?" said Uncle Lem. "Well, that's nice to hear—not too often I—"

"Actually not," Grammy went on. "But you'll do. Now where's that no-good nephew of yours?"

"Nail on the head," said Uncle Lem. "Exactly why I'm here. Good to be on the same page right from the get-go. Doesn't always work out that way, I can tell—"

Grammy's voice rose. Now she was back to her old self for sure. "What are you talking about?"

"Why, Snoozy, ma'am. My nephew—not my only nephew, by any means, why, I've got three locked up at this very moment, just to account for the incarcerated nephews—and your employee. Snoozy sent me to fill in for the rest of the shift, plus the next day or two. Three tops." He caught an expression on Grammy's face and hurried on. "And don't you worry, ma'am. I'll work for the same wages as Snoozy, not a penny more, despite me having so much more experience on the business side of life."

Grammy's mouth—and Birdie's—both seemed to have fallen somewhat open. And what was this? My mouth, too? I took advantage of the moment to give my muzzle a good, thorough lick. Neither Grammy nor Birdie thought of doing that themselves. Sometimes ol' Bowser's way ahead of the game.

"Lem?" Grammy said, her voice quiet in a way I knew meant danger.

"Ma'am?" said Lem, in a bright, unaware-of-danger kind of tone.

48

"Where—is—Snoozy?"

"At this particular moment in time, ma'am? Or in a more general—"

"NOW! Where is Snoozy right now, this very second."

Uncle Lem raised a hand, like someone blocking a thrown object. "Why, where I just left him. No way they'd be finished so soon."

"Finished with what?"

"His new tattoo."

"He's getting another one?" Birdie said.

"Sizable," said Uncle Lem. "But Matisse thinks there's room on his chest to squeeze it in."

"Lem?"

"Ma'am?"

"You stay here."

"That was my plan. Gonna sell my butt off, don't you worry. You know the LaChance family motto."

"I don't," Birdie said.

"Turn it into lemonade," said Uncle Lem.

I smelled no lemonade, no lemons. What was going on today?

Joe Don Matisse's World Famous Tattoo Parlor and Spa was in a little strip mall on the road out of town, not the main road but the other one—that led into farm country and then petered out. We started in—Grammy, Birdie, me—but by the time we were actually inside, somehow it was me in front. I'm lucky that way.

My first time in Joe Don Matisse's World Famous Tattoo Parlor and Spa, but I'd seen Joe Don around town. A hard dude to forget: so enormous, and with such an enormous shaved head that it seemed too enormous for that enormous body. And don't forget the tattoo of a snake on his shaved head, a snake that meant business, fangs extended and tail coiling down to disappear in his huge beard. Not the snake's huge beard, of course—I mean Joe Don's huge beard.

Joe Don was at his workstation, bent over a customer in the chair, a customer with his back to us. The tattoo pen looked tiny in Joe Don's huge, meaty hand. He glanced up.

"Miz Gaux? This is a surprise. Although why, come to think of it? I did a lovely little butterfly on a ninety-three-year-old lady from over in Houma just the other day."

"Then the world's gone mad," Grammy said. "I want Snoozy. Snoozy! On your feet and make it snappy!"

The customer raised her head over the headrest of the operating chair and turned our way. Her head—meaning this wasn't Snoozy. And not only that: She was someone we knew, namely Mrs. Roux from Roux's Drugs.

"Why, hello, Claire!" said Mrs. Roux. "Birdie—how are

you, darlin'? And no leaving out the handsomest pooch on the bayou."

Hadn't I just heard that very thing somewhere else? No problem—it never got old. My tail hit top speed in no time flat, stirring up the air inside Joe Don's place in the nicest way, cooling things off and spreading inky smells all around. Plus hints of blood, no missing that.

"Um, yes, well, hello indeed," Grammy said. "But . . . but where's Snoozy? I was told he was here, treating himself to one more ever-lovin'—here on company time, is what I mean."

"You were told right, Miz Gaux," Joe Don said, "although the company time aspect is news to me. Fact is, we were right in the middle of our pièce de résistance when Snoozy had to up and go. When I say 'we' it's because I consider the customer to be an equal partner in my art, the living canvas, if you catch my drift."

"Oh, Joe Don," Mrs. Roux said, "that is truly beautiful."

Joe Don tapped his chest, right over his heart, one of my favorite human moves. "And although this particular canvas is only half done, I could show you the design sketch if you're interested."

"Design sketch?" Grammy said.

"Yes, please," said Birdie.

Joe Don turned Birdie's way and blinked. "Uh, Birdie? How old would you be now, exactly?"

"Going on twelve."

"Hmm. Technically too young to actually be inside a tattoo establishment in this jurisdiction."

"I'm not getting a tattoo," Birdie said. "Although—"

"Don't even go there, young lady!" Grammy said.

"As for technicalities," Joe Don went on, "no point in getting bogged down in them." He picked up a big sheet of thick paper, brought it over. "Here's the design."

We looked at the design, which turned out to be a pencil drawing.

"A shark?" Birdie said. "You're tattooing a shark on Snoozy's chest?"

"By request. Specifically a bull shark. Note the huge head, hefty snout, and that mouthful of long white sharpies. And those killer eyes! Had to be a bull shark, Snoozy said. We did some back and forth on whether it should be in profile or straight on. Ended up going with straight on, like it's comin' atcha. There are times for subtlety in art, but there are also times to bring the hammer. With a bull shark, you bring the hammer."

"Snoozy requested a bull shark?" Grammy said.

"A bull shark with a lopsided grin," said Joe Don.

"A lopsided grin? Why?"

"The lopsided grin part or the whole concept?"

"Either. Both."

"Couldn't tell you, ma'am," Joe Don said. "In this business, you don't ask. Did Leonardo ask Mona Lisa why she was smiling like that? Don't want to kill the moment."

"How come it says 'Mr. Nice Guy' at the bottom of the page?" Birdie said.

Joe Don laughed. "Just thought I'd name the critter."

"You tattooed 'Mr. Nice Guy' on Snoozy's chest?" Birdie said.

"No, no—that's just on the sketch. Although, when Snoozy comes back to finish up, I might run the idea by him."

"And when would that be?" Grammy said.

"Day or two, depending."

"Depending on what?"

"Snoozy didn't say. He just said depending."

Mrs. Roux piped up. "That's true. Heard it myself."

Grammy turned to her. "You were here?"

Mrs. Roux gestured toward a couple of chairs in the corner. "Waiting my turn. But then Snoozy's ride showed up and honked."

"Hate to stop when the juices are flowing," Joe Don said, "but the customer is always right."

"Snoozy's ride?" Grammy said. "Who are we talking about?"

"He didn't say. Just said he had to split and would be back in a day or two."

"Depending," Birdie said.

"Yeah, depending."

"For goodness' sake," Grammy said. "Did you see who was driving the car?"

"A green pickup, actually," Joe Don said. "Moss green—I'm particular when it comes to color description. But from where I was, by the chair, I couldn't see the driver."

"Me neither," said Mrs. Roux. "But it was a pickup, all right. The kind a serious fisherman would drive, maybe the commercial type."

"Why do you say that?" Grammy said.

"On account of all the nets and buoys and traps in the back," Mrs. Roux said. "I spotted those details as they drove off. I've always had an eye for details."

"Which explains the eagle," Joe Don said.

"What eagle?" said Grammy.

"The eagle Joe Don's putting on my shoulder this very morning."

"Like it's sort of perched there," Joe Don said. "What we call trompe l'oeil. Care to see the sketch?"

■ ■ ■

"What's trompe l'oeil, Grammy?" Birdie said as we drove back across town. "Something Cajun?"

"More like just plain French," said Grammy. "It means 'fool the eye.'"

"That *oeil* sound is hard to make."

"Just put your lips like so—like you're getting ready to sneer."

Birdie made a very strange face and said "oeil, oeil, oeil, oeil" a number of times.

"Enough," said Grammy.

I was with her on that. It was starting to drive me crazy.

We passed the turnoff to the Lucinda Street Bridge, where Wally Tebbets always parked his food truck. I caught a glimpse of Wally—a sweaty man with an apron around his middle and a do-rag on his head—hard at work behind the counter. Junior was lying in the grass nearby, gazing at the sky. I heard Wally yell something at him, but Junior didn't seem to hear.

"So," Grammy said, "not too hard to deduce what's going on here."

"With Junior and his dad?" said Birdie.

"Where did you get that notion? I'm talking about that good-for-nothing Snoozy. What can we deduce?"

"Not sure I know what deduce means, Grammy."

"Like Sherlock Holmes."

"Not sure I know who he is, either."

"Good grief. What do they teach you in school? Don't they make you read anything?"

"Sure—we read lots."

"Like?" said Grammy, then quickly added, "Forget it—I don't want to know. Sherlock Holmes was a storybook detective. He was great at deducing—meaning figuring out what was going on from a handful of clues. Follow?"

"Yes, ma'am."

"Then what's happening with Snoozy?"

"Maybe he decided the shark tattoo was a bad idea after all and texted a buddy to come rescue him."

There was a silence. Grammy glanced over at Birdie. Then she reached out and rumpled Birdie's hair. That was a first! I had no idea what was going on, and neither did Birdie.

"What, Grammy, what?"

"Not a thing," said Grammy. "Stay just like that."

"Like what?"

"Never mind. Here are the clues. A two-bit, corner-cutting charter boat captain name of Deke Waylon comes looking for Snoozy. Then we find out some big shot from up north is putting out a fifty-thousand-dollar bounty on this bull shark. A bull shark that doesn't exist, but ignore that for now. After that comes Snoozy, all eager to add a bull shark tattoo to his gross collection—a bull shark with a lopsided grin. Followed by Snoozy taking off in a pickup full of commercial-style fishing gear."

"Deke Waylon hired Snoozy to help him catch Mr. Nice Guy?" Birdie said.

"There is no Mr. Nice Guy, no bull shark of any kind up the bayou!" We pulled into Gaux Family Fish and Bait. "But yeah, that's the deduction."

"This is all because of how good Snoozy is at finding fish?" Birdie said.

"Yup," said Grammy. "Proof that some higher power can be pretty careless when it comes to handing out talent."

"How come, with all his talent for finding fish, Snoozy never got rich?"

"Because," said Grammy, "you have to get off your butt. Talent isn't enough. In fact, it's worse than nothin' for them that don't get off their butts."

We piled out of the car. None of Grammy's windows go up anymore, so piling in and out's a snap for me.

"Do you think Deke Waylon will split the bounty with Snoozy, fifty-fifty?" Birdie said.

"Bounty? Ain't gonna be no bounty. There's no bull shark! For heaven's sake! Did you not get enough sleep last night, child?" Grammy's eyes shifted, like she'd had a new thought. "No bull shark," she said again, but much more quietly. I myself had enjoyed a very nice sleep the night before. A special farewell steak dinner for Mama and then beddy-bye. I paused inside my head, came very close to figuring something out, actually . . . deducing? Deducing something on my own! Wow!

We went into the store. Uncle Lem stood behind the counter, a cigar stuck in his mouth. He seemed to be counting stacks of money.

5

DID I MENTION THAT LEM'S CIGAR WAS long and thin, the kind called a stogie? Lem twisted his lips around it in funny ways, moving the cigar back and forth across his mouth, almost like he was fixing to chomp on it. Ever spotted a cigar butt in the gutter, snapped it up for a quick taste test? My advice to you: Don't!

"Hey there, boss lady," Lem said. Or something like that. With his mouth so busy on that stogie, Lem was a little hard to understand. "Get everything all sorted out with the Snooze?"

"Lem?"

"Ma'am?"

"What's all that cash?"

"Ah, cash," said Lem, blowing out a huge smoky cloud. My coat was going to smell cigary for days. "Cash on the barrelhead, big green, dead presidents. Although, come to think of it, Hamilton wasn't a president. Or was he? What do they tell you in school, Birdie?"

"Well," said Birdie, "I'm not sure we've gotten to that part yet. I think Grammy wants to know—"

"About that money!" Grammy interrupted. "ASAP!"

"Not much to say," Lem told her. "It's yours." He pushed the stacks of cash closer to Grammy. "Or more accurately, the property of Gaux Family Fish and Bait, depending on how you do your books."

"But . . . but where did it come from?" Grammy said.

"Sales. What I'm here for. Actually, just one."

"One sale? What on earth did you sell?"

"Take a guess."

Grammy and Birdie scanned the store. "I don't see anything missing," Birdie said.

"Heh, heh," said Lem. "Didn't come from in the store. Come from the storage shed, out back."

"You sold the Entire Wilderness Camp in a Box?" Grammy said.

"What's that, Grammy?"

Lem checked a sheet of paper. "'The Entire and Complete Deluxe Wilderness Camp—in a Box That Turns into a Genuine Pioneer Outhouse,' to give it its full name."

"But how did you even know it was there?" Grammy said.

"Snoozy told me all about it. Said the thing's been in that shed since 1972."

"Worst darn product I ever took on," Grammy said. "Practically bankrupted me. Someone actually bought it?"

"Very nice tourist couple," Lem said.

"Tourists from where?" said Grammy.

"China."

"China?"

"I think so. Very nice couple but they didn't speak any English. We used sign language!"

Grammy gazed at Lem. He shrugged in an aw-shucks sort of way. "How come they didn't pay with a credit card?" Grammy said.

"I told them we prefer cash. That's right, isn't it? Certainly how we LaChances roll, going way back."

"Well, yes," Grammy said.

"But how did you tell them if they don't speak English?" Birdie said.

Lem raised his hand, rubbed his thumb and finger together. "Universal language for moola."

Grammy thought for a moment or two. "Good job, Lem."

Lem smiled and puffed out another smoke cloud.

"Maybe we should celebrate," Birdie said.

"Sounds like a plan," said Lem. "How about we—"

"Gettin' ahead of ourselves," Grammy said.

An ice cube arced through the air and fell right into my mouth. No one could toss ice cubes like Nola Claymore, Birdie's best friend—and therefore mine, too. We sat on the shaded porch of Claymore's General Store, Birdie and Nola sipping cold drinks, me chewing on ice cubes.

"Is Junior going to be famous someday?" Birdie said.

"Only if he robs a bank," said Nola.

"He thinks he's a genius."

"Tell me about it."

"So how come you agreed to do this stupid song project?"

"Music, girl!" Nola said. She picked up her guitar. "And what if we actually win and get on the radio?"

"I'd be scared out of my mind."

"Me too. But it goes away as soon as you start performing."

"How do you know?"

"All the rock stars say so." Nola tossed me another ice cube, not even looking. Bull's-eye! "Do you think dogs get nervous?"

Hey! Dogs? This was interesting. I waited to find out what nervous was. Meanwhile, they were both watching me. That made me kind of . . . nervous? Wow! I hadn't had to wait long.

"Nah," Birdie said. "Bowser's Mr. Confidence."

I went back to chewing ice cubes and feeling pleasantly cool all over. Nola strummed her guitar.

"So what's our song going to be?" she said. "We've got maybe an hour."

"Impossible."

"Adele wrote 'Skyfall' in ten minutes."

"Then let's take a break," Birdie said.

Which must have been funny in some way, because she and Nola started laughing. What a lovely sound! The way those two different laughs mixed and matched, leaned away from each other and bent back in! Was that the song? If so, it was going to be a big hit.

All at once, Birdie sat up straight. "Hey! I think I have a title."

"Give," said Nola.

"'Mr. Nice Guy.'"

"Huh? What's Mr. Nice Guy?"

"More like who," Birdie said. "Although it turns out Mr. Nice Guy doesn't actually exist."

"Lost me, sister."

Birdie started up on a long story all about Snoozy and Grammy; Mr. Kronik and his kid, Holden; Joe Don Matisse and Mrs. Roux; salt water and freshwater and in-between water; and all sorts of other stuff, some of it vaguely familiar—like deducing and a corner cutter named Deke Waylon. But what was the question? Who was Mr. Nice Guy? A pelican, maybe? I got the feeling I was pretty close.

Nola picked out some notes on the guitar. Not pretty, maybe, but something about them sent a little jolt down to the tip of my tail. *"Are you real, Mr. Nice Guy?"* she sang.

Birdie's eyes lit up, and she sang, *"Mr. Nice Guy, Mr. Nice Guy,"* in a way that sent another jolt down my tail. It actually met the first one coming back, halfway. What a feeling!

"Or are you a bad, bad dream?" Birdie sang on.

While Nola took over the "Mr. Nice Guy, Mr. Nice Guy" thing.

Then they sang together, Nola handling the low part and Birdie the high—kind of just the way they'd laughed together, if you get what I mean.

"Are you real, Mr. Nice Guy?

Mr. Nice Guy, Mr. Nice Guy,

Or are you a bad, bad dream?

Mr. Nice Guy, Mr. Nice Guy, Mr. Nice Guy."

They stopped singing. Nola's hands went still.

"Well, well," she said.

"Well, well," said Birdie.

"It's a start."

"Now what?"

"We need another verse. Maybe two. Then a middle part. After that we can use the first verse again."

"How do you know all this?"

"Junior told me."

"He couldn't actually be a genius, could he?"

"Only in Upside-Down World."

"Upside-Down World?" Birdie said. "Sounds like another song."

"Message to Adele," Nola said. "Clear the track."

Who was this Adele person they kept talking about? Today was already confusing enough without her horning in.

"Mr. Nice Guy's a great white shark?" said Junior. This was later that day—a hot one, folks were saying, for the time of year, whatever the time of the year happened to be. We—meaning me, Birdie, and Nola—had met Junior at the swimming hole, a sort of side pool of the bayou not too far from the Lucinda Street Bridge. Nola brought her guitar, Junior brought a tambourine and some leftovers from the food truck, Birdie brought cold cans of limeade, her favorite drink, and I brought me.

"Not a great white," Nola said. "A bull shark."

"Which doesn't exist," Birdie said. "And it doesn't matter."

"The shark's just the inspiration," Nola said.

Junior nodded. There was something in that nod that— for one tiny moment—made Junior look much older. "I like it already. Sing."

"Sing?" said Nola. "Like you're some kind of dictator?"

"I'm not a dictator," Junior said. "I'm the producer. And I said please."

"That's a lie," Nola said.

"Okay. I'm saying it now." Junior was back to looking like his normal self, or even younger.

Nola and Birdie exchanged a look, a sort of look they had that made me think they were talking to each other, even when they weren't. Then Nola reached for her guitar, picked out those strange sounds that sent vibrations down my tail, and they leaned their heads together and sang "Mr. Nice Guy."

Junior sat back and clapped his hands. "Love, love, love it," he said. "We're ninety-nine percent there."

"Yeah?" said Birdie.

"Well, maybe ninety or so. Math's not my strong point." He picked up the tambourine. "Lyrics—no problem. I couldn't have done better myself. Tune? Pretty good. Just on that last 'Mr. Nice Guy' on the chorus, Nola? How about trying a quick chord change from the F up to F-sharp? Might give it a . . . I don't know. Like this."

And Junior sang, *"Mr. Nice Guy, Mr. Nice Guy, Mr. Nice Guy,"* and on that last one I got the tail jolt again.

"Plus," said Junior, picking up the tambourine, "I think the whole thing should be much faster." He began shaking the tambourine—*boom shick shicka, boom shick shicka*, real quick, and Nola started strumming, also real quick, and then they sang, the girls doing all the singing except for when Junior joined them on the "Mr. Nice Guy, Mr. Nice Guy" part.

"How'd that go?" Nola said.

"Let's find out," said Junior, and he took a device from his cargo shorts pocket. Human have lots of devices, way too many, in my opinion. This was a little bigger than phone-size and much thicker, with a mesh covering.

"You're pretty sneaky, Junior," Nola said.

"I'm a producer." Junior pressed a button on the device and "Mr. Nice Guy" started up. Sometimes when humans get really interested in something, they go very still, and this was one of those moments, a moment for listening real hard.

"Hey!" said Nola.

"Not too shabby," said Junior.

"Let's try it again," Birdie said. "I can do better."

They did it again, and again, and once more, and then finally Birdie said, "Okay. In the water, everybody."

Everybody was wearing swimsuits under their T-shirts and shorts, except for me, of course. No clothing of any kind for ol' Bowser, unless you count my collar, a lovely leather collar that had smelled of cattle when Birdie first bought it, but now was all me.

Not the point. The point was that with nothing to take off, I should have been first into the water—and I'm the type who likes to be first, no doubt about it—but swimming is different. When it comes to swimming, I let the humans go ahead: much easier to keep track of them that way. Don't get me wrong. I give them time to have some fun, more than enough, from my point of view.

"Hey!" said Junior as we splashed around in the bayou. "What's Bowser up to?"

Birdie swam closer. "Herding. He's herding you back to shore."

"But I don't want to go back to shore."

"He always herds the weakest swimmer first," Nola said.

"You think I'm the weakest?" Junior said.

"By far. You're so skinny you can barely stay afloat."

"Race you."

We raced to shore. Nola won, with me next, sort of on top of Birdie for some reason, and Junior last by plenty. He pulled himself up on the bank, huffing and puffing. Nola was hopping up and down and tapping the side of her head, the way humans often do after swimming, don't ask me why.

"Well," Junior told her, "that's a surprise."

"What is?" said Nola.

"You winning."

"Why is that?"

Junior shrugged. "Because, like, swimming. You know what they say."

It got very quiet down there by the swimming hole. "No, Junior, I don't," Nola said. "What do 'they' say?"

Junior tried to meet her gaze, but could not. "Sorry," he said. "I didn't mean that."

"Then why did you say it?" Birdie said. Hey! She sounded real angry. That hardly ever happened with Birdie. Had Junior done something bad? I sidled over in his direction, just in case he had a mind to . . . I didn't know what. But suddenly starting to cry? I wasn't ready for that, and neither were Birdie or Nola. They looked real surprised.

"I don't know," Junior said, tears on his cheeks. "It's . . . it's the kind of thing my stepmom would say. Not me. Also, she can't stand music. There's no music in the house anymore, and my dad won't . . ." He cried some more.

Finally, Nola held up her hand. "Okay, okay," she said.

Junior wiped his face with his sleeve, turned back into his usual self quite speedily. "Friends?" he said.

"Don't push it," Nola said.

Junior looked like he was going to say something—possibly pushing it, whatever that meant—when from out in the bayou came an enormous splash. We all turned to look, but there was nothing to see except ripples. In fact, you couldn't call them ripples. They were more like waves, gliding fast across the water and curling up the bank of the bayou, practically at our feet.

"Must have been one big fish," Birdie said.

"Like what, Birdie?" said Nola.

"Or a meteor," Junior said.

"Huh?"

"A meteor—from outer space."

A meteor from outer space? I had no clue. Also I was distracted by a new smell in the air. It reminded me of Grammy's turtle soup, which I'd sampled once when . . . when no one was around. Let's leave it at that.

Meanwhile, Nola was saying, "Why don't you dive down out there and check it out?"

"Me?" said Junior. "How about we eat instead?"

He opened the cooler. I was first in line, maybe unnecessary to point out.

"Checking it out?" Birdie said the next morning. "Not a bad idea—plus a chance to try some of that free diving Grammy was talking about." Grammy had already left for work, and Birdie was washing the dishes in the kitchen at 19 Gentilly Lane. I was lying on the floor by my water bowl, zoning out. All in all, a promising start to the day.

"Do you think washing dishes was the connection?" Birdie went on. "Water reminding me of water?"

Birdie had lost me completely. Sometimes when you're lost the best thing to do is have a cooling drink, so that was what I did, lapping up just about all the water in the bowl. Whoa! Water. And hadn't Birdie just been mentioning water? Suddenly, everything was water! I started panting.

"The reason you're panting, Bowser, is because you're not drinking enough water. You're dehydrated, just like Grammy."

What was this? I was like Grammy in some way? And why was Birdie telling me to drink? Hadn't I just been drinking? I stood over my bowl, mouth open, doing pretty much nothing. I didn't even realize Birdie had left the kitchen until she came back, carrying her swimming goggles.

"Let's go."

That broke the spell. I gave myself maybe my all-time most energetic shake and beat her to the door.

Not long after that, we were back at the swimming hole. It was a cloudy day, and on cloudy days the bayou is dark gray instead of blue. Birdie put on her goggles and waded in the water. "You stay, Bowser. I'll be right back."

Birdie swam out toward the middle of the bayou. I

jumped in and swam after her. By the time I caught up, she had stopped and was gazing down, her face in the water. She didn't notice me. That was a bit bothersome. I was about to lay a friendly paw on her shoulder when she suddenly dove down just like a duck, headfirst, and disappeared below the surface.

I peered down and watched her blurry shape going deeper and deeper. Was this a good idea? No! The next thing I knew I was swimming down after her. The water got colder the deeper I went, colder and murkier. I picked up the pace, which was right around when Birdie started coming up, not fast, maybe on account of the fact that she seemed to have something pretty big in her hands. Was she actually struggling, her cheeks puffed out, her legs kicking maybe a little wildly? I couldn't have that, so I twisted around, got myself under her, and herded her up to the surface and then right back to the shore in my most no-nonsense way.

We climbed out of the water, Birdie stumbling a bit. She dropped the heavy thing she'd brought up from the depths of the bayou. It lay in the grass. We gazed down at it, me and Birdie. A turtle shell, darkish green and spiky? Yes, and a very big one, although . . . although this was only part of it. The rest, maybe a whole half, was gone, leaving a rough, jagged edge, like some huge saw blade had gone at it in a rough and clumsy way.

With her foot, Birdie flipped the shell over on its back. Something flopped out, but not all the way, since it was partly still attached. At first I made no sense of it, and then I did. It was the head of the turtle—a very big head, all bloody, and one eye gone.

Birdie backed away. I barked and barked.

6

GRAMMY! LOOK WHAT WE FOUND!"

Grammy was under the tin roof behind the store, where we've got our workshop. Small-engine repair is one of our specialties, in case that hasn't come up yet. Grammy had the cover off an outboard and was probing around inside with a screwdriver. She looked up. Uh-oh. Her face was grayish again.

Birdie laid the turtle shell on Grammy's workbench. The bloody head came loose. "Good grief, child." Grammy picked up the head and tossed it over her shoulder, straight into the bayou. She wiped her hand on her apron and glanced at the shell.

"Snapper—specifically the alligator snapping turtle, biggest one we've got."

"It's part alligator?"

"'Course not! What a notion!"

"It's just called alligator cause it's big? Like the alligator gar?"

"Guess so," said Grammy. "Folks here have gator on the brain, if you haven't noticed."

"But what happened to it?" Birdie said. "The way it got cut in two like that."

"Ran into a prop," said Grammy. "Where'd you find it?"

"Down at the bottom of the swimming hole."

Grammy's gaze shifted to the goggles, perched on Birdie's head.

"Who was with you?"

"Where?"

"Don't be smart. Who was with you at the swimming hole? Bottom's thirty feet out there, measured it myself."

"Uh, Bowser," Birdie said.

"You were diving alone at the swimming hole? Going down thirty feet? Wrestling that godforsaken shell out of the muck?"

"Not alone, Grammy. With Bowser."

"Didn't I say don't be smart? Dogs don't count. Why on earth—" Grammy stopped, put her hand on her chest, then sat down heavily on the workbench stool.

Birdie hurried over, put her hand on Grammy's back. "Grammy?" And then came a lot of activity—Birdie running into the store, running back out with a bottle of water, Grammy drinking—but don't rely on me for the details, because I was stuck on *dogs don't count. Dogs don't count?* What did that even mean? Poor Grammy. She wasn't herself.

But as Grammy downed the bottle of water, her usual self returned, sip by sip. I could actually smell the change happening, as though a fresh breeze was driving off a dust cloud. I went closer to her, and sat, my tail wagging back and forth across the cement floor in an encouraging way. I was waiting for her to say, "How ridiculous! Must have been out of my ever-lovin' mind. Of course dogs count! Dogs count big-time! How about a treat?"

None of that happened. Grammy did finally notice me. "What in heck do you want?"

I tried to remember. Meanwhile, she gave me a quick scratch between the ears, right on the spot I just can't reach. Grammy's a surprisingly talented scratcher. We were good, Grammy and me.

Lem came through the back door. What was this? He had another big wad of money in his hand?

"Hey, boss," he said. "Some problem?"

Grammy rose. "Problem?"

"From the way Birdie come runnin' in and out, I thought—"

"There's no problem," Grammy said. "What's all that money?"

"All yours," said Lem. "Or property of the corporation, depending on how you do your books, like I said before. Happy to look over the books any time you like, by the way."

"Why would I want you to do that?"

"I'm kind of an expert when it comes to doing the books," Lem said. "Leastwise, I was taught by an expert."

"Who would that be?"

"A former cell—uh, roommate—was what you might call a wheeler-dealer on Wall Street. I could tell you stories—there was one day when he owned every single pork chop west of the Mississippi."

Hold it right there. Which side of the Mississippi were we on, again? The Mississippi came up a lot in conversation, so I was pretty sure we were close. A river, wasn't it? Like the bayou, except bigger? All at once, I came up with the most brilliant plan of my life. The first time I saw the Mississippi I'd sniff the air. If I caught a whiff of pork chops, I'd stay where I was. If not, I'd swim across. Wow! That was me? Life only got better.

Meanwhile, Lem was balancing the wad of cash on the workbench. Grammy picked it up and counted it.

"Whoa! What did you sell? Everything in the store?"

"Heh, heh," said Lem. "Not one single thing that's in the store."

"Lem?" Grammy said. "Best not be telling me you're up to no good."

"Me, boss? Those days—if they ever even happened for real, and I'm none too sure on account of . . . history. My own personal history having some blank spots, if you see my meaning."

"Get to the point," Grammy said.

"You'll never guess," said Lem. "I rented out *Bayou Girl* for a New Year's Eve cruise. Fireworks, champagne, all you can eat, music—six grand, cash in advance and on the barrelhead."

"But we don't do New Year's Eve cruises," Birdie said. "We don't do any party cruises at all."

Lem laughed. "Which is how come I said she'd never guess." His phone buzzed. Still laughing, he pulled a phone out of his pocket and squinted at the screen. His laughter faded away. "Hmm," he said. "Text from Snoozy. Wants me to come get 'im." Lem looked up. "Guess my time as your employee is done. Feels like we're just gettin' started, don't it, ma'am?"

Grammy smiled. Hey! That didn't happen often. Her teeth, although kind of yellow, were all there, and nicely shaped, to my way of thinking. "It does," she said.

"Been a pleasure, ma'am. Love dealin' with the public— talkin' about the innocent retail public. Not like the wholesalers in the crawfish business, nickel-and-dimers every last one."

"I do some wholesaling in the crawfish business," Grammy said, her smile vanishing real quick.

"And I always say," Lem hurried on, "there's only one decent wholesaler in the crawfish business, and that's old lady—and that's Miz Gaux." He held out his hand. They shook.

"Where are you picking him up?" Grammy said.

"Snoozy? Down near Baie LaRouche. Place called Shakey's Shakes."

"Haven't been there in thirty years," Grammy said.

"Shakey's Shakes?" Birdie said. "Can I go, Grammy? They're supposed to have the best shakes in the whole state. I'll bring you one."

"Whether you can go or not depends on Lem."

"Be a pleasure," said Lem.

"Strawberry," Grammy said.

This was hard to follow. Bottom line? We were splitting. Although my name may not have come up, it didn't matter. Where Birdie goes, I go.

Lem's pickup wasn't the most dinged you see in these parts, but close. He and Birdie climbed in—Lem using his hands to give his limpy leg some help—and I hopped onto the pickup bed in back. Nothing like riding in the back of a pickup! We were barely on the road when another pickup went by, also with one of my kind in the back. A she, as it happened—we know that from just the tiniest whiff in my world. We barked at each other furiously, she and I, even though she looked sort of nice to me, and I'm sure I looked the same to her. Or even better! So what was with all the angry barking? You're asking the wrong dude.

Meanwhile, the back window of the cab was open, and I could hear Birdie and Lem talking up front.

"Wanna hear a story about your daddy?" Lem was saying. "From back when I coached him in Pee Wee football?"

What had I heard about that? Something or other: Lem had been a football star way, way back, long before the bad leg and all the barrooms. And Birdie hadn't known her daddy, so anytime someone had a story about him, she was all ears. Not really, of course, her ears being on the small side, and beautifully shaped. When it comes to hearing, they don't work very well, true for every human I'd ever met. And let's not even start on their noses. What are they for? *Sniff, sniff. Do you smell smoke, honey?* And meanwhile, the house is burning down around them!

"Yeah," Birdie said. "Sure."

"He was probably right around your age," Lem said. "How old are you again?"

"Going on twelve."

"Twelve, huh? Yeah, your daddy was right about that. Pee Wee As. He grew into a big, strong man, as maybe you know, but back then he was small, not much bigger than you."

"No?"

"Nope. But strong for his size. So guess what position he played?"

"Wide receiver?"

"Center. Smack dab in the middle of the mayhem up front. And on defense he was the noseguard, same thing."

"Didn't he get pushed around?"

"Everybody gets pushed around in football. It's them that push back and don't stop pushing back who are the real players. But that's not the story. Back then things weren't so . . . what would you say? Integrated, maybe? Weren't so integrated in these parts."

"Integrated?"

"Like you and your pal. What's her name?"

"Nola."

"Yeah. Back then that woulda been kinda unusual. On that Pee Wee A team—state champs—we had just the one black kid, J. B. A little guy, not even as big as your daddy, fast and shifty. But the star of the team was the quarterback, name I won't say, since he's still around. Big and strong, already man-size. And he had a thing about J. B.

Just wouldn't stop. Not when I was around, you understand—it was sneakier. Then one day it did stop, just like that." Lem snapped his fingers. "Know how come?"

"No."

"Because—this was from the janitor, who happened to be passing by the locker room after practice—your daddy walked right on up to that great big star of the team, looked him in the eye, and said, 'That's enough with J. B. It's over.' And it was."

I couldn't see Birdie's face at that moment, only the back of her head, her neck, her square shoulders. She was sitting up very straight and very still.

All our countryside is pretty low, but now we were driving through the lowest I'd seen. The land around us got more and more watery, and finally, through a gap in the trees up ahead, it disappeared completely, and there was nothing except endless blue. We made a turn, drove through a very small town, worn-out-looking and not nearly as nice as St. Roch. Down on the docks, a big commotion seemed to be going on. A bunch of dudes were shouting at each other, waving their arms. One or two had boat hooks in their hands, nasty hooks that slashed through the air above the heads of the angry men.

"What's going on?" Birdie said.

"Nothin' good," said Lem. He drove on, through some woods at the edge of town, and stopped in front of a strange building. It was shaped like a tall glass, with a flat roof and a giant sort of straw poking through.

"Shakey's Shakes," Lem said. We got out—me hopping, as you probably guessed—and went inside. I was first somehow, even though I paused on the way to lift my leg against a small bush, a bush where others of my kind had done a lot of leg-lifting—some of it very recent, judging by the freshness of the smells.

There were different smells inside—chocolate, vanilla, strawberry, raspberry, caramel, cherry, cream, and those were just some. I left out bananas, for one thing. Wow! I loved it already. Shakey's Shakes had some tables and chairs, all empty. The only person there was a big woman behind the counter. She wore a white cap and a white uniform, and had a frosty scoop in her hand.

"Welcome to Shakey's Shakes," she said. "I'm Mrs. Shakey. What'll it be?"

"Any idea what's happening down at the dock?" Lem said.

Mrs. Shakey frowned. "Darn bounty's got all the watermen stirred up. There's some that thinks they own personal stretches of the Gulf all to themselves. How's any good gonna come out of this?"

"I hear you." Lem glanced around. "Supposed to be meeting someone. Gentleman name of Snoozy LaChance."

"Don't know him," said Mrs. Shakey.

"Little shorter than me. Younger, too," said Lem. "Thinner."

Mrs. Shakey shook her head.

"He's got lots of tattoos on his arms," Birdie said. "All fish."

"Different fish or the same?" Mrs. Shakey said.

"All different," said Birdie.

"Sounds like an interesting type," Mrs. Shakey said. "But he hasn't been here. I'd notice something like that."

"We'll wait," Lem said. He and Birdie ordered shakes.

"And how about our four-footed friend?" Mrs. Shakey said. I waited to find out who that might be. "Just so happens," she went on, "I bake doggy biscuits on the side."

Who's luckier than me? No-body, baby. No-body. We sat at a table—me on the floor, the humans in chairs, our usual procedure—and had a nice quiet time, Birdie and Lem with their shakes and me with the best biscuit of my life, and then another, and possibly one more after that.

Lem took out his phone. "Shoot him a text." We waited some more. "Typical," Lem said after checking his phone and checking it again. "All LaChances are on their own time of course—point of pride—but Snoozy's . . ."

". . . in his own century?" Birdie said.

Lem laughed. "Remind me to tell him that. In his own century!" That started him up on laughing again, and he was still at it when two little kids—younger than Birdie—came in, the girl with a fishing pole, the boy with a net. Mrs. Shakey looked at them in surprise.

"Back so soon?" she said.

"There was yelling, Ma," said the girl.

"Yelling?"

"Men yelling," said the boy. "And maybe a gunshot."

"A firecracker," the girl said.

"Gunshot," said the boy.

They pushed and shoved.

7

WE STOOD OUTSIDE SHAKEY'S SHAKES:
Mrs. Shakey, her two kids, Lem, Birdie,
and me. One of the kids pointed down
a path that led into some scrubby woods. "Thataway,"
he said.

"Near the dock?" Mrs. Shakey asked.

"Past it," said the kid.

"Firecracker," said the girl.

The kids glared at each other.

"Snap out of it!" said Mrs. Shakey.

One of the kids said something smart and Mrs. Shakey
said something about "upside the head," but I never found
out what came next, because we were already on the trail,
me in the lead, picking up the scents of the two kids, followed by Birdie and then Lem, limping along in the rear.

"Are we still in the parish?" Birdie said as we entered
the scrubby woods.

"Think so," said Lem. "Why?"

"Maybe we should call the sheriff."

"To report a possible gunshot in the middle of nowhere?

Folks called in stuff like that around these parts, the sheriff would be doin' nothin' else."

We walked on. I heard waves breaking gently not far away and smelled the sea.

"Does Snoozy have a gun?" Birdie said.

"Does he own a gun?" Lem said. "Expect so. But he wouldn't be carrying, if that's what you mean. Guns are something that forgetful types might leave behind in the wrong place, lead to unpleasant complications. Snoozy knows his limitations."

"Yeah?"

"Actually, no. He's a LaChance, after all."

Were they talking about Snoozy? That was interesting, because a third human scent had started mixing in with the scents of Mrs. Shakey's kids. The smell of a human male, with hints of barbecue sauce, beer, ink, and a kind of cologne maybe called Mr. Manly, that Grammy couldn't stand. Only one person I knew had that very special smell: Snoozy. How fresh was it? Not quite as fresh as the smell of the kids, but certainly from today. Night changes the smell of everything, a fun fact you maybe didn't know, and the old smell never quite comes back.

Up ahead, the way was blocked by mangroves—don't ever try to make your way through a mangrove tangle—but the path curved, and all at once we were on a beach.

Not a beach, if what you mean by a beach is a soft, sandy strand. What we had here was a little patch of mud and weeds, with mangrove barriers on both sides. Leading out into the water from this weedy mud patch of a beach was a dock—if two rotten old boards held together here and there with duct tape could be called a dock. These boards, floating on the water, extended a surprisingly long way out.

"Hmm," Lem said.

"The kids said the yelling came from past the dock," Birdie said. "But past the dock is all those mangroves."

"Right," said Lem. "So maybe somebody should walk on out to the end of this here dock and take a look-see. Someone light, to my way of thinking, on account of the workmanship being on the rickety side."

Birdie looked down at me. We made eye contact. I love making eye contact with Birdie. I concentrated hard, making my best eye contact ever. "You stay here, Bowser. I'll be right back. There's a good boy."

She stepped out onto the dock. I stepped out right behind her. Had she just told me something? I tried to remember what it might have been. Something about being a good boy? Nothing else came to me, but I didn't spend much time on it because I was busy getting ahead of Birdie, our procedure always having me first, as I'm sure you know by now. Not an easy thing to do, on such a narrow dock, but ol' Bowser can be pretty dazzling when it comes to footwork, and no one fell in the drink. At least not completely in, if completely in means getting your head wet.

Me and Birdie, both of our heads nice and dry, stood at the end of the ramshackle dock, out on salt water—no missing that smell, probably even detectable by humans. The dock rose and fell in a gentle way, like it was resting on the chest of some huge, breathing thing. Birdie turned to scan the shoreline past where the dock began. After not too far, the mangroves suddenly opened up, and we saw another muddy and weedy beach. Something grayish lay on the beach, not moving.

"Lem?"

"Yeah?"

"There's another beach."

"Yeah?"

"Just past those mangroves."

"Uh-huh."

"With something on it."

"What kind of something?"

"I don't know. It's . . . it's not moving, Lem."

Lem bent down and rolled up his pant legs. He waded out into the water, slow and limping. We went back to the start of the dock, stepped into the water, and caught up to him. First it was very shallow and I was mostly walking. The bottom was mucky, sucking at my paws, and with the occasional sharp thing poking through. Then it got deeper and I swam—much better, keeping some space between me and the bottom. Lem was up to just past his knees, and Birdie to her waist. They were very quiet, not saying anything. The water made rippling sounds around us. Otherwise, no sound at all—kind of strange, like we were all alone in the world.

We passed the last gnarly mangrove roots, which came right out of the water, just another annoying thing about mangroves—shouldn't roots stay down in the ground, not bothering anybody?—and came to the second beach. Right away I picked up the scent of death—not long-ago death, or death a few days old, which is the worst, but recent death, more than a day and less than two. And now we got a closer look at the grayish figure on the beach.

"Oh my god," said Lem.

"Snoozy?" Birdie said, and she covered her mouth.

Lem began to run, a painful-looking hobbling run, but then he slowed down.

"Just a fish," he said. "Whew."

I'm a big fan of humans, don't get me wrong, but they can be a little . . . slow at times. For example, I'd known from the get-go not only that this figure, sprawled in a curving shape, was not alive, but also that it was not a person. In fact, a fish of some sort. If you can't pick up the dead fish scent, what can you smell?

We stood around this fish—not even the size of a human adult, more like the size of one of Mrs. Shakey's kids.

"A shark?" Birdie said.

"Yup."

"Not . . . not Mr. Nice Guy?"

"Huh?" said Lem, looking at her in surprise.

"Um, just the name we have for the shark—the one that all the fuss is about, if it's real. The shark, I mean."

She'd lost me. The shark lying in front of us was real, no doubt about it.

"This here's no maneater," Lem said. "Not a bull shark at all—what we got is a nurse shark. See those two thingies—barbels, they call 'em—between the nostrils? That's the giveaway. There's nurse sharks all over the Gulf, but they ain't no threat to fish nor fowl."

"No threat to fish?" Birdie said. "What do they eat?"

"Well, fish," said Lem. "But not in a threatening way, if you get what I mean."

"Um," said Birdie. She gazed down at the dead shark. "Hey! What's that?" She pointed at . . . at what looked like a small hole, round and red, midway between the shark's eyes, which were open but dull and lightless.

Lem bent down. "Bullet hole." He shook his head.

"Someone just shot it and left it here?" Birdie said. "Is that what the kids heard?"

"Can't think of no other explanation—although how that coulda happened on the beach . . ." Lem turned and looked out on the water. At that very moment, a pirogue came put-putting from behind the mangroves, a pirogue being a small open boat we have in these parts, and put-putting on account of the tininess of the outboard motor. Sitting in the stern, one hand on the control stick, was an old guy with thick, snowy-white hair and a nose that reminded me of an eagle that had once landed on the roof of Gaux Family Fish and Bait. I hadn't relaxed until that bird had taken off and disappeared in the blue.

The old man cut the engine and let the boat coast on up to the beach. He climbed out—grunting a little but moving pretty well for such an ancient dude, kind of how Grammy moved, in fact. He walked toward us, his feet bare and nicely shaped, to my way of thinking. Then he gazed at each one of us in turn, including me. That's something I've noticed about humans: Some include me and some don't.

He gestured with his chin at the shark. "I'm assuming none of you had anything to do with this."

Lem shook his head. "We just got here." He indicated the direction we'd come from. "Kid back there thought maybe he'd heard a shot, so we come out to investigate. And . . ." He knelt and pointed out the bullet hole. "Which turned out to be true—hearing the shot, I mean."

The old man glanced at the shark. "When was this shot fired?"

"Don't know, exactly," Lem said. "But not too long ago."

With his eagle nose—even eagle face, actually, the face of an old eagle-human type—this man looked impatient to begin with, but now he ramped it up. "Today? Are you talking about today?"

"Oh, yeah, sure. We stopped for shakes and then—"

The old man made a slicing movement with his hand. "Then the supposed shot had nothing to do with what happened to this shark. It should be clear to even the untrained eye that death occurred at least a day ago, possibly two or three." Hey! This old dude and I were . . . of one mind? Is that the expression? Something about it bothered me. I did not want to share a mind with anybody, certainly not him. Birdie, maybe.

"This shark," he went on, "was shot out on the water and the body drifted in." He did that slicing thing again, this time harder than before. Was he angry about something? "And what's more, it's a disgrace," he said.

"Well," Lem said, "some of the fishermen get a little slap-happy when it comes to—"

"It's got nothing to do with fishermen!" The old man's voice started out loud and booming, but then cracked and finished in a wispy way. He coughed and pounded on his chest, all his impatience now turned on himself.

"Um," Birdie said, "what has it got to do with? Sir?"

The old man turned to her. "What's your name?"

"Birdie."

He nodded, that little repeating nod humans do when they like something.

"And I'm Lem," said Lem. "Pleased to meet you, Mr. . . ."

"Longstreet," said the old man. "Henry Longstreet. As for your question, Birdie, this has nothing to do with fishermen. It's all about the bounty hunters. Bounty hunters! I could strangle them with—" Mr. Longstreet's hands, old and worn, but big and still powerful-looking, curled into fists. He took a deep breath. "The real culprit, of course, is the arrogant ignoramus who put the bounty out there in the first place. Do you know how many sharks I've seen in the past two days with bullets through their heads? Four! And now five, counting this one. Two nurses, one fine-tooth, one blacknose, one spinner, all ocean-going only."

"No bull sharks?" Birdie said.

"Oh?" said Mr. Longstreet. "You know something about this? No, not a single bull shark. These cowboys are shooting at anything with gills and checking after the fact.

But even if they were killing bull sharks, it would make no difference."

"Because there's no way a bull shark could get up the bayou as far as Betencourt Bridge?" Birdie said.

"Where are you getting that information?"

"My grammy," Birdie said.

"With all due respect, your grammy happens to be dead wrong."

Birdie took a step back. I stayed right with her.

"The fact is," Mr. Longstreet continued, "there was a documented bull shark sighting in Montville seventy-three years ago, and Montville's seven miles up the river from Betencourt Bridge. Documented by my father, with photos he took himself."

"He was a photographer?" Lem said.

"A marine biologist," said Mr. Longstreet. "As am I, or was. I'm retired. Now my interest is in conservation."

"So you're saying Holden Kronik really was attacked by a bull shark?" Birdie said.

"Who is Holden Kronik?"

"The boy from Betencourt Bridge."

"The one whose father is paying the bounty?"

"I guess so."

"You guess so. Do you know these people?"

"Not really," Birdie said.

Around then was when I noticed a pair of sunglasses lying on the deck of Mr. Longstreet's pirogue, beside the fuel tank. Sunglasses on boats are no surprise, but these sunglasses had an unusual Croakie attached, a Croakie decorated with tiny mermaids. I edged closer to the pirogue.

Meanwhile, Mr. Longstreet was saying, "Must have been a scare for the boy, if indeed he had an encounter with a bull shark. But I take it he wasn't hurt, so no harm done. Maybe next time he'll be more careful."

"More careful?" Birdie said. "How?"

"How? By respecting the territory of others."

"Huh?" said Lem. "Who is these others?"

Mr. Longstreet turned his eagle nose in Lem's direction. "Other creatures, Len."

"Lem," said Birdie.

Mr. Longstreet didn't seem to notice. "Other creatures with whom we share this planet. Think of where it ends if we just start killing off sharks willy-nilly. Which, by the way, is pretty much happening in certain parts of the world. Ever heard of the food chain? What happens if a single link is wiped out?"

I knew food, which I loved. I also knew chains, which I hated. I tried to fit the two things together, and could not. Which didn't bother me in the slightest! I'm lucky that way! Maybe it's because what I like in life is action. I was in action at that very moment, in fact, reaching my head into the stern of the pirogue and grabbing those sunglasses with the mermaid Croakie. Why? Because . . . because . . . Does there always have to be a why?

I trotted back over to the others. They were so busy with their discussion—somewhat boring, if you want my opinion—that they didn't notice me. I was fine with that for what seemed like the longest time. Then, when I couldn't stand it anymore—and I'm sure you would have felt the same, in my place—I pressed myself against Birdie's leg, not too hard.

"Bowser!" she said, perhaps stumbling a bit, for reasons unknown to me. "What are you—"

Her gaze went to the mermaid Croakie.

8

BOWSER?" BIRDIE SAID. "WHAT YOU GOT there?"

She knelt in front of me, reached for the sunglasses. I let her have them. Most of the time I put up resistance when people try to take something from my mouth, maybe a lot of resistance, but usually just for fun. Not this time, of course: We're dealing with Birdie here. She's not people. Well, a person, yes, but not people, if you get my meaning. I'm not sure I do, myself.

"This looks like one of Snoozy's Croakies," she said.

"Yeah," Lem said, giving it a close look, "the mermaid one. Snooze got it online at All Things Croakie dot com—he's a preferred customer."

"Where did you find these sunglasses, Bowser?" Birdie said. "What are they doing here?"

Or something like that. I was too busy wagging my tail to really concentrate. I could just tell I'd done good. What a feeling!

"He didn't find 'em here," Lem said. "Not on the beach. He took 'em outta the pirogue—I seen him do it."

Wow! Was Lem on the ball today or what?

He and Birdie turned slowly toward Mr. Longstreet.

"Mr. Longstreet," Lem said. "What're these here sunglasses with this here particular Croakie doing in your pirogue?"

Mr. Longstreet looked down his eagle nose at the sunglasses. "I haven't the slightest idea—"

"You don't know how the sunglasses got into your own pirogue?" Lem said.

"I'm saying no such thing. If you'd let me finish this time, I was about to say I haven't the slightest idea why it's any concern of yours."

I felt Birdie go very still beside me. Did we like this Longstreet dude or not? I was starting to think not, and my teeth were thinking the same way, meaning they were starting to feel a little bitey. That's bad, I know, and I got a grip right away.

"Well, now," said Lem, standing up straighter, a very big guy even if not in the best of shape, "those sunglasses belong to my nephew Snoozy, and that makes it our concern."

Mr. Longstreet had dark eyes, not a shiny sort of dark, but more faded. Now they shifted sideways. That's a human thing for when they're listening to something in their head.

"What makes you think that these sunglasses—" At which point Mr. Longstreet made a grab for them, followed by Birdie doing something amazing: She put the sunglasses behind her back, out of Mr. Longstreet's reach! And Mr.

Longstreet himself did look amazed, if not in a happy way. He licked his lips and continued. "What makes you think they belong to this supposed nephew of yours?"

"That there mermaid Croakie, like I was just saying," Lem told him.

"And I recognize the sunglasses, too," Birdie said, holding them up so Mr. Longstreet could see, but out of his reach. "With the gold lenses—they're his favorites."

"So maybe now," Lem said, "you can explain how you got them."

"I found them," said Mr. Longstreet. "And you can have them." He turned toward the pirogue, like he was thinking of shipping off.

"Sure thing, since they're my nephew's and all," Lem said.

"But wait!" said Birdie. "You still didn't tell us where you found them!"

Mr. Longstreet paused and spoke over his shoulder, not looking back at us. "You both seem . . . rather stirred up about something." Now he turned. "Why don't you explain—explain politely—what this is about."

"As an old teacher of mine used to say," Lem said, "politeness is a group activity." He looked Mr. Longstreet in the eye. Mr. Longstreet looked him back the same way. Lem looked down. I wasn't happy to see that, although I didn't know why.

100

But then Birdie spoke up, and I was back to being happy. Just her voice does that to me, even if she actually sounded a bit annoyed at the moment.

"We're looking for Snoozy," she said. "That's what this is about."

Aha! I'd actually lost track of that. Lem seemed glad to hear it, too: His head came up, and he didn't look so . . . so beaten, if that was the word.

"Yeah," he said, *"Mister* Longstreet. Snoozy texted us to swing down and get him, but now he ain't where he's supposed to be, and a possession of his turns up on your vessel. So where'd you find those sunglasses?"

Mr. Longstreet gazed at Lem, then at Birdie, last at me. "Can the dog behave himself in a boat?"

What was this? Me? Boats? Me and boats went together like . . . like the very best going-together things in the whole world! Or better!

"Bowser's his name," Birdie said. "And he's a natural-born sailor."

"Then get in the boat," Mr. Longstreet said, "and I'll show you where I found the wretched sunglasses."

When it comes to boating, I prefer the bow seat. Isn't it meant for me and my kind? Bow wow, after all. Enough said.

So on this particular boat ride, we had a problem right from the get-go, what with Lem taking possession of the

101

bow seat before I even had a chance. That left me in the middle with Birdie—her sitting on a big cooler and me on the deck—and Mr. Longstreet in the stern, driving the boat. But as the shore slipped away and I watched the water sliding past, I forgot whatever it was that I'd been upset about. There's something about being on the water—especially calm water, like this—that takes your mind off everything. I felt pretty darn good, close to my best, and when I'm close to my best I can hear and smell things like you wouldn't believe. For example, I could hear Birdie's heart beating, a lovely *thump-thump, thump-thump*. As for smells, I knew there was a baloney sandwich in that cooler. Baloney with tomato and mustard, on rye. There was also . . . a gun? There's no missing that, not with a nose like mine.

"Bowser! What's that growling about?"

"Don't tell me he's going to be sick all over the boat!" said Mr. Longstreet.

Sick? What a weird idea! Then I got it: Sick meant pukey! Here's a funny thing: Even though I hadn't felt the slightest bit pukey in I don't know how long, all of a sudden now I did! I leaned down toward the deck and—

"Bowser! Don't you be sick!"

—and . . . and got it together. In no time at all I was back on top of my game.

Meanwhile, we were on the move, chugging around a

point with one tall tree at the end—a tree with a pink flamingo in it, by the way, always a nice sight—and on our
way to a nearby island, low and green. Two trees grew on
this island, and as we got closer I saw there was a pink
flamingo in each. How interesting! Although I didn't know
why. I barked once or twice—or maybe a few more barks
than that, but nothing crazy—just to see if I could get
those flamingos to take off.

"Bowser!"

But they stayed put.

Mr. Longstreet swung the pirogue sideways, cut the
engine, and drifted us into what must have been the remains
of a dock, just a single thick beam with rusty bolts sticking out of it. Birdie and I hopped out, Lem tossed her the
bowline, she tied up, and then Mr. Longstreet led us up an
overgrown path, with me in the actual lead. I picked up
Snoozy's scent right away—his Mr. Manly cologne was like
a trumpet blast, if that makes any sense—and also another
smell, namely of gasoline and bait worms. Gasoline and bait
worms are part of my life, of course, in my co-ownership
role at Gaux Family Fish and Bait, but at this moment the
smell was actually reminding me of something else. I tried
to think what.

We rounded a bend and came to an old tumbledown
stone hut, roofless and covered in vines.

"What is this place?" Birdie said.

"Could go all the way back to the pirates," said Lem. "Made of ballast stones—we got no stones like these around here. We used to search for buried treasure in huts like this, back when I was a kid."

Mr. Longstreet, standing behind Lem, gave him a long look, his head tilted slightly to one side. My guess is humans do that when they're seeing something in a new way, but I could be wrong.

"Did you find any?" Birdie said.

"Nope."

Mr. Longstreet pointed to the open doorway. "The sunglasses were inside."

Were the sunglasses some sort of treasure? That was as far as I could take it.

We went inside. And we weren't the first, which I knew from the strong smell of pee. A lot of peeing had gone on in the hut—was that the treasure?—yes, lots of peeing by all sorts of creatures, four-footed and two-footed. How could I possibly lay my mark on all those pee places? Plus this might not be a good time for doing that—hard to tell, one of those judgment calls, whatever those were.

Also, in this hut we had the scent of creatures with no legs at all, meaning snakes. But no snakes on the scene at the moment, the snaky smells being much too old. The Mr.

Manly and gasoline and bait worm smells weren't old at all. What else? Broken bottles, empty cans, cigarette butts, and a busted-up old wooden crate.

"That's where I spotted the sunglasses," said Mr. Longstreet. "Beside that crate."

We gazed at the crate. Not much to see, in my opinion. Birdie went over, picked it up, and looked underneath. "I already did that," said Mr. Longstreet.

Birdie didn't appear to hear him. All her concentration was on the end of one of the crate's broken boards. "This crate got smashed up recently," she said.

"Huh?" said Lem.

"See the broken ends? The wood is kind of fresh-looking. All the rest of the crate is old and moldy."

"Hey!" said Lem.

"Young Miss Sherlock," said Mr. Longstreet. First I'd heard of Miss Sherlock, but I didn't like the way he'd said her name. "And what do you deduce from that?" he went on.

Birdie turned to him. The sunshine coming through the open roof lit up her head in a lovely way. "I think we should talk to Sheriff Cannon."

"Oh?" said Mr. Longstreet, so tall that his own head was almost poking through where the roof would have been. "And why is that?"

"Maybe . . . maybe Snoozy's in trouble."

Snoozy in trouble? That caught my attention—maybe on account of those busted boards of the crate. It wasn't the freshness of the break—I couldn't make anything of that— but on account of the very faint smell of blood coming off the jagged ends. Blood mixed with Mr. Manly.

Meanwhile, Lem was raising his heavy shoulders. "What kind of trouble, Birdie?"

"I don't know."

There was a silence. In a dim corner I saw a big bug struggling in a spiderweb. The spider, even bigger, was moving toward it along the silvery strands of the web, in no particular hurry.

"Trouble?" Mr. Longstreet said. "Come around to the back and I'll show you something that's actually troubling."

We followed him out of the hut and around to the back. Two weathered posts stood behind the hut, holding up a crosswise plank. Hooks were nailed to the plank, just like on the display boards you see on all the docks around here, where the charter boat dudes show off the fish they caught. And there were fish hanging on these hooks, too— all sharks, to my eye, none of them real big.

"Not a bull shark among them, you'll notice," Mr. Longstreet said. "This is a crime." His face had gone pale and he seemed to be shaking a bit.

"The law says you can't kill sharks?" said Lem.

"It most certainly does, for some species at some times of the year."

"Any of these?" said Birdie. "At this time of the year?"

Mr. Longstreet gave her a look, annoyed but thoughtful, too. "What's your last name?"

"Gaux."

"Gaux?"

Birdie nodded.

"Where are you from?"

"St. Roch."

Mr. Longstreet's eyes got a faraway look. Then he blinked, turned to Lem, and said, "There are crimes against the law and crimes against morality. It's a lawman's job to stop lawbreakers. It's everybody's job to stop morality breakers."

"Lost me," Lem said.

I was totally with Lem on that. Was Birdie lost as well? Mr. Longstreet was still gazing at Lem. Birdie's eyes were on Mr. Longstreet. Did they seem lost? Not to my way of thinking. They looked watchful.

There wasn't much talk after that. We piled back into the pirogue. The smell from Mr. Longstreet's cooler was stronger now, especially the baloney part. I wanted that baloney real bad! In a perfect world Mr. Longstreet would have said, "Hey, Bowser, want to share my baloney sandwich? Heck, take the whole thing!" But he didn't. This was a great world, but not perfect. I could also still pick up the smell of the gun in the cooler. I shouldn't leave that out.

Mr. Longstreet dropped us at a dock near Shakey's Shakes. We were walking to Lem's truck when Birdie said, "Grammy wanted strawberry." She went in to get it. Lem looked my way. "She's got a head on her shoulders, Bowser. We need to visit with the sheriff."

Hey! Lem was talking to me? Not many humans did: Birdie, of course, Mama sometimes, Grammy not very often, and usually when I was in trouble. And now Lem. Welcome to the club, Lem! As for what he'd said—namely that Birdie had a head, just like everyone else I knew— well, maybe he'd come up with something better the next time.

9

SOME FOLKS GOT MORE EDUCATION THAN others," Lem said on the ride back to St. Roch. Same setup as before, with Birdie up front in the passenger seat of the pickup and me on the truck bed in back, the rear window open. I was lying down, feeling a bit sleepy, with their voices flowing over me in a pleasant way.

"Like Mr. Longstreet?" Birdie said.

"Uh-huh. The educated type for sure. On the other hand, there's me."

"I don't understand—you went to college. You played for the Ragin' Cajuns."

"But I wasn't in class a whole lot. And the classes I signed up for . . . well, I probably couldn't have told you what they were even back then. My life was football. I was headed to the NFL and that was all what mattered. And then I blew out my knee and reverted back to the parish. A cheap shot but the zebras never threw the flag. I . . . I got hung up on that for a long time. Talkin' about decades, Birdie."

"Because it was so unfair?"

"I guess."

"Not just the bad call," Birdie said. "I meant the whole thing."

"Got a head on your shoulders, no doubt about it. But here's what I finally figured out. Can't get bogged down in what-if. Gotta have dreams, sure. One foot in the dream world, but the other on solid ground. So get an education, Birdie."

"I already know I'm not going to the NFL," Birdie said.

Lem laughed and laughed. "Don't let me forget that one," he said. And then, "My memory's not what it should be. I've had botha my feet in the booze for way too long."

"Oh," Birdie said.

"But what I finally realized is that I got a lot out of football anyways—worth doing just for itself, you see what I mean. And the moment that hit me, the bottle lost its power. Haven't touched a drink since."

"That's great, Lem. What made you realize?"

"Just popped into my head. I was with Snoozy, actually. He was goin' on and on about somethin' or other—baboons, maybe—and that was when it came to me. Worth doing for itself, Birdie. Left my drink unfinished in the glass."

"When was this?" Birdie said.

"Week ago Friday," said Lem.

Birdie was silent. Or maybe not, but my mind was now totally on baboons. I knew them from the Nature Channel, which me and Birdie watched sometimes, especially on rainy days. Were baboons in the parish? We had problems.

First thing back in St. Roch, we swung by Snoozy's place. Snoozy had a double-wide in a trailer park on the outskirts of town, a trailer park that had gone out of business, so he had a lot of scrubland all to himself. "Biggest landowner in town," he said, "and I don't even own it!" Birdie always laughed when he said that, so I'd heard it many times.

"Be one sec," said Lem, getting out of the truck. He knocked on Snoozy's door. "You back? Snooze?"

No answer. Snoozy had one of those lawn gnomes out front. Lawn gnomes scared me at first, but now I've gotten used to them, even find them useful at times. This particular lawn gnome was smoking a pipe. Lem reached into the bowl of the pipe and took out a key. He went back to the double-wide, unlocked the door, and walked in.

"Snoozy? Snooze?"

Lem disappeared into the shadows beyond the open doorway.

"Snoozy?"

Silence.

Lem came back, got in the truck. "No sign of him." We drove off. I had hoped to get a bit closer to the gnome. Maybe next time. Meanwhile, I wriggled around a bit, made myself comfortable. That's one of my best skills.

111

■ ■ ■

I woke up feeling . . . well, superb, if you must know. That's what a nap will do for you. I rose, gave myself a good shake, enough to rattle things around in my head, get the show on the road up there. First things first: Where was I? Hey! Still in the back of Lem's truck, a bit of a surprise. Right away I smelled Grammy's strawberry shake, packed with ice in a small Styrofoam box up front. We were no longer moving—in fact, seemed to be back in the center of St. Roch, parked in front of the sheriff's office, with its blue light over the door. And on their way inside were . . . Birdie and Lem! By some strange accident, they appeared to have forgotten me. No problemo. These things happen. I hopped on out of the pickup and bounded across the sheriff's lawn—snagging an old tennis ball on the way— and squeezed inside the doorway just in time.

Birdie turned. "Bowser!"

Did she sound happy to see me? I thought so and dropped the tennis ball at her feet, just to let her know I was on top of things.

"Help you folks?" said a woman at the front desk.

"Like to see the sheriff," said Lem, nodding at a closed door with a star on it.

"He's in a meeting—shouldn't be long." She gestured toward some seats. We sat down, me nice and comfy under

Birdie's chair. On a nearby wall were photos of a bunch of tough-looking customers. Birdie scanned them.

"There's a couple I know," Lem said, "just at a glance."

"Which ones?" Birdie said.

Lem raised his hand to point, but just then the door with the star opened and out came a short and thick-necked dude with a neatly trimmed beard, sort of backing out. He seemed familiar and then—boom! The name came to me: It was Mr. Kronik from up at Betencourt Bridge. What a sharp memory I had all of a sudden! I'd rattled things around in my head but good!

Did we like Mr. Kronik? I kind of thought we did not. And also that the sheriff didn't feel especially buddy-buddy with him, either, so it was a bit of a surprise when Mr. Kronik said, "And nice talking to you, too, Sheriff. Keep in touch."

Then came the voice of the sheriff. "Will do."

The sheriff's door closed. Mr. Kronik had taken a few steps across the waiting room when he noticed Lem. He showed no reaction to Lem, but then his gaze found me and Birdie. First his eyebrows went up, like he recognized us and was kind of surprised. Then his eyebrows went down and bunched together in the middle—not the most pleasant look, considering the bushiness of those eyebrows, kind of like the chubby caterpillars you see in these parts.

His mouth opened like he was going to say something, but he did not.

"Hi, Mr. Kronik," Birdie said.

"Uh," said Mr. Kronik, "Birdie, was it?"

"Yes, sir."

He glanced at Lem and then at me. There's a scent humans give off when they're uncomfortable around me and my kind; not the smell of sweat, exactly, more like sweating is about to start up any second. Mr. Kronik was giving off that scent.

"You—you just hang out here?" he said. "Or what?"

"No, sir," said Birdie.

His mouth did that opening-and-closing thing again. Then he said, "Have a nice day." He headed for the front door.

"Say hi to Holden," Birdie said.

Mr. Kronik went out, perhaps closing the door harder than necessary. The woman behind the desk rose and entered the sheriff's office.

"You know that guy?" said Lem.

"He's the one who put up the bounty," Birdie said.

"Yeah?" said Lem. "I wonder what . . . Hmm."

Meanwhile, behind the sheriff's closed door, the woman was speaking real softly so no one in the waiting room could possibly hear. No humans, anyway. But that didn't include ol' Bowser, who heard her say, "Lem LaChance is out there. With a youngster—a friend of Rory's, I think. She's got a dog with her."

"Birdie Gaux?" said the sheriff, also very softly.

"Yeah, I think so."

"What do they want?"

"Didn't say."

"Good grief."

"Want me to tell them you're busy?"

The sheriff sighed.

Then the woman came out, gave us a big smile, and said, "You can go on in."

"Well, well," said Sheriff Cannon, rising from behind his desk, a big smile on his face. Big smiles on top of one another! We were having a good day. "What a nice surprise! Take a seat."

We sat—except for me. I felt like standing. No reason, unless you count the faint scent of a ham and cheese sandwich rising from the sheriff's wastebasket. Not a whole sandwich—nothing to get excited about—but even a tiny scrap beats no food at all.

"Would you look at that tail wagging away," said the sheriff.

"Happy to see you," said Birdie.

Sure, think whatever you want. I eased my way closer to the wastebasket.

"Haven't, uh, seen you in some time, Lem," the sheriff said. "Professionally, that is. How's the crawfish business?"

"Same old, same old," said Lem.

"Got wind of some missing traps up in Cleoma."

"Wouldn't know nothin' about that."

"Good to hear," said the sheriff. "So what can I do for you folks?"

"It's about my nephew."

The sheriff laughed. "Come to bail one out? I've got what—three? four?—in lockup at this very moment."

"Three," said Lem, not laughing. "And this ain't about them. It's about Snoozy. He's gone missing."

The sheriff wiped his mouth, getting it back in non-laughing position, and slid a writing pad into place. "How long's he been missing?"

Lem thought. "Hard to say exactly. Depends on . . ." He turned to Birdie.

"Snoozy left yesterday—to join up with one of the bounty hunters."

"Bounty hunters?" said the sheriff.

"Mr. Kronik's bounty." Birdie nodded to the door. The sheriff sat back, his eyes kind of watchful. "Today he texted Lem to come get him down in Baie LaRouche but—"

116

"Yeah, right, exactly," Lem said. "At Shakey's Shakes."

"—he wasn't there," Birdie finished up.

"How long ago was this text?" said the sheriff, writing on the pad.

"Three, four hours," Lem told him.

The sheriff looked up. "So Snoozy's been missing for three or four hours?"

"We haven't actually seen him since yesterday," Birdie said.

"But that doesn't count, since he's been heard from since then. I've got to follow procedure, Birdie, and procedure says no one can be labeled officially missing until twenty-four hours are up. Besides, Snoozy's a grown man, capable of taking care of himself."

"But—"

"And also capable—no disrespect for Snoozy, who's always been a law-abiding citizen, give or take—of changing his mind about a rendezvous on account of who knows what. Agreed?"

Lem sat there for a bit, then slowly nodded his head. Birdie just sat there.

"Birdie?" said the sheriff. "You're not with me here?"

Birdie folded her hands in her lap. I loved that! Although don't ask me why. "The thing is," she said, "some kids heard yelling. And maybe a gunshot."

"A gunshot? Where was this?"

"On the beach—not too far from Shakey's."

"Who were these kids?"

"Mrs. Shakey's kids," said Birdie.

The sheriff wrote some more on the pad, then got on the phone. "Mrs. Shakey? Hey, there, ma'am. Sheriff Cannon up here in St. Roch. How's your day goin'?" He listened, laughed, and said, "I hear you. Got word of a possible gunshot down your way. Your kids heard it, maybe? Something like that." He listened again. I could hear Mrs. Shakey on the other end.

"Good lord. Listen, Sheriff. I got two kids. One's the imaginative type, has nightmares and such. The other one the factual type, no imagination whatsoever. Mr. Imagination says he heard a shot. Miss Factual says it was a firecracker. So you tell me."

The sheriff laughed, hung up, put down his pen, and went through the whole imagination-factual thing again, me paying not much attention. By that time, I was right beside the wastebasket, could make out a very small remnant of a ham and cheese sandwich. But way more interesting was the fact of what the wastebasket had hidden from my sight, namely a small cooler. A small cooler with the top off, I might add. And let's add one more detail: There was half a ham and cheese sandwich in that cooler, completely untouched.

"So what I think we'll do," the sheriff said, "is give this

118

another day or two, see if Snoozy shows up, which dollars to doughnuts he will."

Doughnuts? Was the sheriff saying there were doughnuts in the cooler? That just wasn't the case. What we had in the cooler was half a ham and cheese sandwich—no longer actually inside the cooler, strictly speaking—and a can of soda. Doughnuts? Not a one. I began to have doubts about Sheriff Cannon.

"But, Sheriff," Birdie said. "What about Mr. Longstreet?"

"Who's he?" said the sheriff.

"This old man we met down there. Near where the shot went off."

"Firecracker," the sheriff said. He checked his watch.

"But he's against the bounty hunt."

"An environmental type," Lem said.

"And he hates the bounty hunters," Birdie said. "So maybe—"

The sheriff held up his hand in the stop sign. "The state is full of environmental types, as you put it. I'm one myself. Let's not go looking for trouble. We're going to give Snoozy a day or two to come in from the cold."

"What cold?" Lem said.

"It's just an expression," the sheriff said. "So—another day or two. Agreed?"

"All right," said Lem.

"Birdie?" the sheriff said.

Birdie got a stubborn look on her face, not flattering on most humans but very pretty on her. "Are you against the bounty?" she said.

"Huh?"

"Being an environmentalist."

"I am not against the bounty," the sheriff said.

"You're for it?"

"I didn't say that. I'm neutral."

"What's neutral?" Birdie said.

"No opinion one way or the other," the sheriff said. "At this point in time. Although I sure wish some of those guys down on the water would chill out a bit. But for now just tell me you agree to wait a day or two—let's call it two—for Snoozy."

"But what about the sunglasses?" Birdie said.

"Sunglasses?"

Birdie took the sunglasses with the mermaid Croakie from her pocket and laid them on the sheriff's desk. "Snoozy's sunglasses."

"Right," said Lem. "Know Little Flamingo Island, Sheriff?"

"Sure."

"The sunglasses was in the hut. And outside was some sharks hung up on a board."

"Bull sharks?" said the sheriff.

"No."

"And inside was a crate that had gotten smashed up," Birdie said.

The sheriff sat back. "Are these some dots I'm supposed to be connecting? All right, here goes. Snoozy's after the bounty. He kills some sharks down off Baie LaRouche, takes a nap. When he leaves he forgets his sunglasses. Please don't tell me he's never forgotten sunglasses before. I know for a fact he's searched through our lost and found more than once."

"But . . . but the crate," Birdie said.

"What about it?"

"It was smashed up."

"You already said that."

"But recently. The split part of the wood looked fresh."

Hey! I remembered that part. Plus the smell of blood mixed with Mr. Manly.

The sheriff smiled. "You'll be running the FBI someday, Birdie. But I'm missing what you're trying to tell me about that crate."

"I think there was a fight inside that hut," Birdie said.

"Got more to go on than the smashed-up crate?" the sheriff said. Birdie had no answer. "It's not near enough," the sheriff continued. "So—two days. Agreed?"

There was a long pause, and then Birdie said, "Okay."

We went out, closed the sheriff's door, headed across the lobby. What with the closed door and the distance between us I can't guarantee I heard exactly what the sheriff said, but it sure sounded like, "Could've sworn I saved half of that . . ." His voice trailed off in a puzzled sort of way. Poor sheriff: Not everything in life is understandable. I'd learned that myself a long time ago.

There's a rocker in the breezeway between Grammy's half of our place at 19 Gentilly Lane and ours—ours meaning mine, Birdie's, and Mama's. Grammy was sitting in it later that day—the sun sinking behind the tree branches across the street—rocking gently and sipping her strawberry shake.

"Ah," she said. "Hits the spot." She did some more sniffing. "Understand you and Lem spoke to the sheriff."

"Did Lem call you?"

"The sheriff did."

"I don't think he's on top of this, Grammy. Why doesn't—"

Grammy held up her hand. "Hold it right there. What he's saying makes sense—especially since it's a Snoozy situation."

"But—"

"Two days. Then if he doesn't show up, we'll revamp."

"What's revamp?"

"Make new plans. So are we on the same page here?"

"Okay."

"Meaning the exact same page?"

"Yes, ma'am."

"Good." Grammy rocked a bit, the strawberry shake in her lap. Was she about to fall asleep? "Give me a few minutes and I'll fix supper," she said.

"I'll do it, Grammy," Birdie said.

"Oh?" said Grammy, getting more wakeful. "What are you cooking?"

"I could try that vegetarian pot pie Mama likes."

"Tell you what," said Grammy. "Here's ten bucks. Whyn't you head on over to Brick Oven Express and bring us back a pizza."

"Thanks, Grammy."

"Pepperoni, sausage, and what's that ham I like?"

"Prosciutto?"

Prosciutto? I was with Grammy on that. No complaints regarding the partial ham sandwich I may or may not have downed recently, but there was no comparing ordinary, everyday ham with prosciutto. Birdie and I took off for Brick Oven Express—

"Bowser! Slow down!"

—and got there in no time. Birdie placed the order and we went to wait at one of the picnic tables out back. There was one customer already there, a rumply-haired kid with a strange jumble of teeth, some little, some big. Birdie rocked the same jumbly look when it came to teeth, except it worked better on her. But that wasn't the point. The point? The customer was Rory, a good buddy of ours, and son of Sheriff Cannon.

Rory didn't notice us right away. His head was down and he appeared to be staring at nothing. I do that, too! A nice way to relax from time to time, zone out, clear your head. Nothing like a clear head, absolutely empty, to make you feel on top of things. But Rory didn't seem to be having a nice, relaxing time. In fact, he had that brooding look humans sometimes get.

"Hey, Rory," Birdie said.

He looked up. I like to see a lively expression on a human face—the same way a wagging tail is a good thing!—so Rory's face was a bit of a letdown.

"Hi, Birdie," he said.

"Wha'cha doin'?" Birdie said.

"Waiting for a pizza."

"Same."

Birdie sat down across from Rory at his table. Usually when kids meet up, there's a whole buzz of chitchat right from the get-go—like they can hardly wait to get started—but not this time. Rory had a drink in a plastic cup. He swirled the ice around for a bit, and then, still staring into the cup, said, "Junior Tebbets."

"What about him?"

"Heard you and him are cutting a record."

"I wouldn't call it cutting a record. And Nola's part of it, too."

"What would you call it?"

"WSBY's having a song contest. We're entering."

"You and Junior."

"And Nola."

"Uh-huh, sure."

"What does that mean?"

"Nothing." Rory swirled the ice around some more. "You don't think he's a little weird?"

"Weird how?"

Rory shrugged. "He doesn't play any sports."

"Neither do I."

"But you could, if you didn't help out in the store after school. You're fast and you've got a great arm."

Hey! I remembered about Birdie's arm from the day she pitched Rory out of his hitting slump. That was the best baseball I'd ever tasted.

"And anyway," Rory went on, "fishing's your sport— you said so yourself."

"Not sure where you're going with this," Birdie said.

I was with her on that. Truth is, I'm usually not sure where any human is going with anything! With Birdie, of course, you always know you'll end up someplace good.

"Nowhere." Rory raised his cup, downed what was left, including an ice cube or two. All at once he started choking and pounding his chest and staggering around. In other words, something had gone wrong. I was all set to get pretty excited, but Birdie just said, "Ice cube?"

Rory nodded his head kind of frantically and said, "Rrmmgh, rrmmgh."

"Just relax. Breathe through your nose. It'll melt." Birdie didn't even get up.

Rory staggered around some more, maybe trying to do what she'd told him. After a few moments of that, he paused, gulped, straightened, took a deep breath, and said, "Whew." He turned to Birdie. "Uh, thanks."

"No problem."

"Where'd you learn that?"

"Grammy."

Rory sat back down, now looking more like his usual self. "What's the song about?"

"Bull sharks," Birdie said. "Actually, this one particular bull shark that's maybe in the bayou. There's a fifty-thousand-dollar bounty. Heard about it?"

"Oh, yeah."

"'Oh, yeah' meaning . . ."

Now he looked down again. "Can't say."

"Can't say what?"

His voice rose. "If I can't say, I can't say." He looked up and glared at her.

"Fine," Birdie said. "Keep it to yourself." Silence. "Whatever's bothering you."

More silence. Then Rory sighed. "Birdie?"

"Yes?"

"You have to promise not to tell."

"I promise."

"You have to swear."

"I swear."

"That's not an official swear. It has to be on something."

"Like what?"

Rory glanced around. His gaze settled on me, scratching behind my ear and minding my own business. "Bowser. Swear on Bowser's head."

Birdie touched my head and said, "I swear."

Was this some new game? Not very promising so far. I preferred the old ones, fetch, for example.

"I told my dad," Rory said.

"Told him what?"

"That I wouldn't tell anybody."

"Right," said Birdie. "But I swore."

Rory nodded, sighed another time or two, and sort of blurted, "We're moving."

"Where?"

"Betencourt Bridge for now—well, not now, but in the spring. And maybe later to Chicago."

"How come?"

"My dad's been offered this new job. He's not gonna run for sheriff in the spring."

"What new job?"

"The bounty guy you mentioned."

"Mr. Kronik?"

"Yeah. He's doubling my dad's pay to come head up security for all the development he's got going in the state."

"I thought it was just the call center."

"Way more to it," Rory said. "And if everything works out Mr. Kronik might bring him up to Chicago to be on the executive committee of the whole company."

"What's the executive committee?"

"Don't ask me."

Then came another silence. Birdie got all thoughtful. Rory watched her think.

10

LOVED THAT STRAWBERRY SHAKE," GRAMMY said the next morning. "Set me up real good."

It was early, Birdie still in her pajamas, hair all wild and a tiny dried streak of drool on her cheek. Who could take their eyes off Birdie?

"You don't have to come in today," Grammy went on. "There's a two-hour swamp tour that I'll handle, and Lem can watch the store."

"Yeah? You're sure?"

"You're a kid. Kids are supposed to have fun."

"I am having fun."

"I think you're worrying too much."

"I'm not, Grammy," Birdie said. "Um, is there any word on Snoozy?"

Grammy gave her a close look.

"What?" Birdie said. "What?"

"You don't realize what you just did?"

"What did I just—oh!" Birdie started laughing.

Grammy laughed, too. "Proves my point. And if I hear from Snoozy, you'll be the first to know."

Grammy left for work. Birdie and I had breakfast. "Grammy sure looks good today—like that strawberry shake was a magic potion." Birdie went on about this and that for a while—a lovely sound—but I was mainly listening to the *crunch crunch* of my kibble, even lovelier. I was almost done when there was a knock on the door. Normally, I bark in no uncertain terms when someone knocks on the door, but this knock—*bumpity bump bump*—was Nola's. I finished with breakfast in an unhurried way, or at least told myself I would, although the truth is I have only one eating style, namely gobbling up every last morsel as fast as possible.

Nola came in, sat down, spooned herself some cereal from Birdie's bowl. "Junior thinks we should have a name."

"A name for the band?"

"Yeah. I suggested Birdie, Nola, and Junior. No go."

"He wants Junior first?"

"Kind of. What he wants is Junior and His All-Stars. Actually Junior Tebbets and His Personal All-Stars, with all the letters of Junior Tebbets in capitals—at least that's how it was on the napkin."

"Forget it."

"That's what I said. He said think of something better."

"Strawberry Shake."

"Huh?"

"Isn't that better?"

"Yeah," Nola said. "Can't wait to see his reaction when we tell him. Mind if I put a little sugar on this?" She added sugar to Birdie's cereal, helped herself to more. "Almost forgot," she said, talking with her mouth full, not so easy to understand. "That corner-cutting guy? Charter boat captain or something?"

"Deke Waylon?"

"Yeah. He was in the store yesterday, buying a rifle. But Mom didn't have the exact one he wanted. She ordered overnight. He's coming back this morning."

Birdie was on her feet. Was something up? That would have been my guess, but as to what, I had no clue.

Claymore's General Store is a friendly place, sort of like Gaux Family Fish and Bait but much bigger. Also it doesn't smell of fish and bait. There's always a water bowl on the shaded porch out front. I wasn't particularly thirsty, but a single sniff told me that one of my kind had been drinking here and not long ago. That meant he thought the bowl belonged to him! How crazy was that! This particular bowl, like all the other bowls I'd ever drunk from, was mine! Just to prove it once and for all, I lapped up every last drop from that bowl on the porch of Claymore's

General Store. On account of that, I didn't follow Birdie and Nola inside right away. By the time I went through the swinging doors—squeezing through underneath, my go-to method when it comes to swinging doors—Birdie and Nola were standing in front of Mrs. Claymore, a short, round woman with a no-nonsense face but a warm and musical sort of voice that seemed to send the message that a little nonsense would be okay, after all. Kind of a complicated thought on my part, way beyond what I can usually do. So let's skip ahead to what she was actually saying.

". . . Weatherby carbine. Paid cash."

"You mean he's already been here?" Birdie said.

"Left half an hour ago."

"Where did he go?" Birdie said.

"Couldn't tell you," Mrs. Claymore said. "What's up?"

"Kind of a long story," Birdie said.

"About Snoozy LaChance," Nola added.

"Say no more," said Mrs. Claymore. "Bound to make no sense if it's about Snoozy. Let me check the paperwork." She went over to the cash register, thumbed through some papers. "Here we go. Deke Waylon. Got an address down in Baie LaRouche—"

"Baie LaRouche?" Birdie said.

". . . but in case the delivery came in last night, he wanted it brought over to his boat—the *Dixie Flyer*. He had it tied up over at East Bank Marine. Not sure if he's still—"

132

By that time, we were on our way. I had no idea where, but somehow I still managed to stay in the lead pretty much the whole time. We crossed the little square in front of Claymore's General Store—a square with the statue of a soldier in the center, the flowerbeds around it neat and tidy—and headed down Lucinda Street to the bridge. And there, just off to the side, was Wally Tebbets's food truck. The truck had a line out front and Wally, behind the counter, was doing several things at once. Junior sat in a lawn chair on the shady side of the truck, tapping his drumsticks on his knee and chewing gum. He looked up.

"Hey! Guys!"

Birdie and Nola glanced his way without breaking stride.

"We're good on the name?" he called after us. "Junior Tebbets and His Personal All-Stars?"

"Not now," Nola called back.

"Not now you can't talk about it?" Junior rose. "Or not now you're not good on the name?"

"Both," Birdie yelled.

We ran across the bridge, got on the boardwalk that lined the other side of the bayou all the way to the vet's office, and—whoa! Were we on a visit to the vet? I like just about any visit you can name, but not that. Going to the vet always reminds me of my time in the shelter before Birdie came along and made everything right. So I kind of lagged back a little, letting Birdie and Nola get ahead. But I hated that. So I sprinted past them. But what about the vet? I lagged back. Then sprinted. Then lagged back. And was so busy with all that, I didn't notice we'd gone past the vet's place until it was well behind us and we were on a paved path.

"What's with him?" Nola was saying, in that panting voice humans have when they're running.

"Sometimes he gets in a state."

Who were they talking about? No time to get to the bottom of that, because we were just reaching a small marina—parking lot, office, drink machine, gas pumps, boats in slips along the dock. We slowed down, walked from boat to boat along the dock, Birdie checking the writing on the sterns.

"Here we go," she said. *Dixie Flyer.*

I'm not what you'd call an expert when it comes to boats—nothing like Grammy—but when you work at Gaux Family Fish and Bait you get familiar with the basics. *Dixie Flyer* was not a nice boat. Nice boats don't have stray ropes lying all over the place, or sandwich wrappers under the console, or bait buckets standing uncovered in the sun, or a fish half-cleaned near the fishing seats at the back, blood and guts spilled on the deck.

"Kind of messy, huh?" Nola said.

"A floating yard sale," said Birdie. "That's what Grammy calls a boat like this." She turned toward the cabin up front and raised her voice. "Hey! Anybody on board?"

Silence.

"Aren't you supposed to say 'ahoy'?" Nola said.

"Try it."

Nola cupped her hands to her mouth. "Ahoy! Ahoy there!"

Silence. At that moment, Junior came running up, panting and sweating, his Mohawk slumped over to one side.

"Hey," he said. Pant, pant, pant. "What's the hurry? You don't like the 'personal' part? We could go with 'His Hand-Picked All-Stars.' Or—"

"Junior, zip it," Nola said. "This is something else."

"What?"

"Snoozy's disappeared," Birdie said. "He might be on this boat." She raised her voice again. "Snoozy! Snoozy! Are you in there? Are you okay?"

Junior raised his voice even higher, so high it hurt my ears. "SNOOZY! WAKE UP!"

"Never thought of that," Nola said. "But it's so obvious."

"Thanks," Junior said.

Nola yelled, "SNOOZY! WAKE UP!"

Silence.

"Nobody sleeps like Snoozy," Junior said. "Guess we'll have to . . ." And then he took a little jump and hopped on board, one of his flip-flops catching the top rail and falling into the bayou. Junior didn't seem to notice. He headed toward the cabin.

"Junior!" Birdie said. "You can't board someone's boat without permission."

"Yeah?" said Junior, knocking—actually more like pounding—on the cabin door.

No sound from inside the cabin.

"What if it's an emergency?" Nola said.

"Like the *Titanic*," Junior said. "And you have to rescue the girl."

"But—" Birdie said.

By then Junior had turned the knob, opened the door, and disappeared inside. Birdie turned to speak to Nola, but saw something over Nola's shoulder, a sight that made her eyes open wide. I looked in that direction.

What was this? We had company? No doubt about it: A small, wiry dude with long, stringy hair was coming our way. He looked kind of familiar. How come I hadn't heard him? He must have been one of those quiet walkers, rare among humans. That realization got me so close to remembering his name. Then the wind shifted a bit and I caught a whiff of him. This dude smelled fishy. Had to be—Deke Waylon! Wow! Let's hear it for Bowser!

136

Birdie spoke in a strange voice, kind of a loud whisper. "Junior! Junior!"

No answer from Junior.

"Hey," said Deke Waylon, shifting a long, hard case he was carrying from one hand to the other. You see those long, hard cases around these parts from time to time, especially during hunting season. "What's going on?"

Birdie gave him a smallish wave. "We—we're looking for Snoozy."

"Snoozy LaChance? What would he be doin' here?" He gave Birdie a squinty look. "You're the Gaux kid?"

"Yeah," Birdie said. She shot a real quick glance at the cabin. "And . . . because he went on the shark hunt with you, we thought, uh . . ."

"He'd be on board," Nola finished up.

Deke stared at her. "You look kind of familiar."

"Um," Nola said. "So is he on board?"

"Well, now," Deke said, "don't know where you got that idea in your heads."

Birdie tilted up her head. Her face gets kind of hard when she does that. Not really hard, of course: How could a face so beautiful look hard? "From when you came to the store looking for him."

Deke licked his lips. "Right there you jumped to the wrong conclusion. I never met up with that no-good—I never met up with Snoozy LaChance."

Birdie's face got a little harder, a little more beautiful. "But what about Joe Don Matisse's tattoo parlor?"

"Huh? You're makin' no sense."

"Didn't you pick Snoozy up there? Mrs. Roux saw him drive off in your truck."

"Truck?" said Deke, leaning in toward Birdie in a way I didn't like one little bit. At the same time, the cabin door on *Dixie Flyer* opened and out stepped Junior.

He opened his mouth to say something, then noticed what was going on and shut himself up double quick. Nola made a tiny motion, waving him away. Junior backed into the cabin and slowly closed the door.

"I don't own no truck," Deke was saying.

"A pickup," Birdie said. "With lots of gear in the back."

"Makin' me say it again? No one taught you manners? I don't own no truck, no pickup. Don't even own no car."

"You don't own a car?"

"Harley's my ride, now and forever. Any more dumb-ass questions?"

"But then where's Snoozy?" Birdie said. "What happened to him?"

"How in—" Deke stopped himself. His eyes shifted, not a good look, what with how squinty they were to begin with. "Don't ask me," he went on. "But there's certain environmental types all worked up about the bounty."

"Do you mean Mr. Longstreet?" Birdie said.

"Ain't namin' no names," Deke said. "And this confab is now finito."

Birdie and Nola both shot alarmed glances toward the cabin on *Dixie Flyer*.

"Wait!" Birdie said.

"What fer?"

"Um."

"The Harley!" Nola said. "I love Harleys. Can you give us a look at the Harley?" She pointed back toward the marina parking lot.

"What in—"

"A quick one," Birdie said.

"Real quick," said Nola.

"You two out of your minds?" Deke said. "First off, why would I have my Harley here? I'm on the boat. Second, even if I woulda had it, why'd I wanna show it to you? Now, g'wan, scat!" He clutched the long, hard case to his chest, grabbed the rail, and swung himself on board *Dixie Flyer*.

Birdie and Nola looked at each other. Were they scared about something? I tried to think what. Meanwhile, Deke was casting off the bow and stern lines, pulling in the fenders—you learn all this lingo when you're operating a business like Gaux Family Fish and Bait—and turning out to be a real fast mover on a boat. He went to the console, stuck the keys in the ignition, and—

"Hold it!" Birdie said.

Deke looked up.

"Yeah, hold it!" said Nola, adding very softly out of the side of her mouth, "For what?"

"I—I think someone's calling you from the office!" Birdie said.

Deke paused, then glanced at the office. No one was around. In fact, it looked closed, like everybody was on a break. Deke cocked his ear. "I don't hear nothin'." He was right about that. Was it possible Birdie was hearing something I couldn't? Forget it. But did that mean that Deke and I were . . . close, in some way? What a horrible thought! Sometimes when I'm confused, I give myself a good shake and get a fresh start, like it's a brand-new day. I got busy with that on the dock at East Bank Marine.

Deke turned his back on us and cranked the engine. It went *rumble rumble* and *Dixie Flyer* started chugging away down the bayou, making a pretty wake, foaming and bubbling. Nice to see, and also nice that Deke was sailing out of the picture. I've met a lot of boat captains in my time, all of them more pleasant than Deke. So I expected Birdie and Nola to have cheerful looks on their faces.

But they did not. In fact, far from it. They were

watching *Dixie Flyer* shrink in the distance, their faces actually sort of horrified.

"Oh my god," Birdie said.

"What do we do now?" said Nola.

Maybe I was missing something.

11

WE'VE GOT TO RESCUE HIM!" BIRDIE said.

That sounded exciting. Now all I needed was the name of whoever was in trouble and we were good to go.

"But how?" Nola said. "How could Junior do anything so dumb?"

Junior? Junior was in trouble? I gazed at *Dixie Flyer*, now approaching the bend in the bayou. Once around that bend it would be out of sight. Hey! Was Junior on that boat? With Deke Waylon? Probably not a good idea.

"We'll never figure that out!" Birdie said. "We've got to concentrate on what we can do right now!"

"Run after the boat?" Nola said.

"We'd never catch up," Birdie said. "And the path stops at the bend. After that we'd be bushwhacking."

Bushwhacking? When do we start? I took a step or two down the bayou, but no one seemed to be following me. How was I supposed to lead if no one followed?

"What about going after them in *Bayou Girl*?" Nola said.

"I can't take *Bayou Girl* out by myself. So we'd have to explain to Grammy."

"How do they get along—Junior and Grammy?"

"Don't ask."

"Got it." Nola thought. I could feel her thinking. I could also feel Birdie thinking. The thoughts they were having sort of came together and mingled in the air, so much thinking going on that there was no point in me joining in. "What about the jon boat?" Nola said, the jon boat being the flat-bottomed boat we used for the smaller swamp tours.

"I could maybe take that," Birdie said, "but even if we catch up, what then?"

"We'd have to distract Deke somehow so Junior can sneak off."

"But how? Especially since Deke'll be pretty suspicious when he sees it's us. What we need is for Deke to stop the boat and get off for a few minutes."

"What would make him do a thing like that?" Nola said. Then she snapped her fingers, a cracking sound that cut through all those tangled thoughts in the air.

We raced into Claymore's General Store. No one was out front. Nola went behind the counter, flipped through a batch of papers. "Here we go."

"Is there a number?" Birdie said.

"Yup." Nola picked up the phone. "I'll text him." She started tapping away. "'So sorry. Overcharged U. Taking refund to East Bank Marina—$200. CU there!'"

Then we waited. I wasn't sure for what. After not very long, the phone pinged. Nola checked the screen. "He took the bait!"

This was about fishing? I'd kind of suspected that. But no more time to think. The next moment we were on the run again, back across the Lucinda Street Bridge and down the path to the East Bank Marina. Between the office and the boat slips stood some big fuel pumps. We crouched behind them.

Chug chug chug. I heard a boat coming upstream. After a few moments, Birdie and Nola heard it, too. Birdie put her finger to her lips. "Shh, Bowser. Not a peep."

No worries there: A peep is a sound I wouldn't even know how to make. We peeked around the corner of the last fuel pump—the three of us pressed together nice and close, me in the center of things, which always felt best—and saw *Dixie Flyer* come into view. Deke stood at the console, his long, stringy hair all over the place in the breeze. He steered the boat into the same slip he'd had before, came to a stop that seemed a little too hard to me, but I was used to real smooth boaters like Birdie and Grammy. *Make that boat just kiss the bumpers when you come in, child,* Grammy always said. Maybe Deke was in a hurry. He jumped onto the dock, whipped a rope around a cleat, then came walking quickly in our direction. We ducked back behind the fuel pumps, out of sight.

Birdie and Nola seemed to be holding their breath. I wondered why: It looked pretty uncomfortable. Deke was a very quiet walker, but I could hear him going by the pumps on the other side, moving fast. A few moments after that, I heard the office door open and close.

We tore out from behind the fuel pumps, glanced back at the office. Through the window we could see the blurry figure of Deke talking to some other blurry figure. We ran to *Dixie Flyer.*

No sign of anyone. The cabin door was closed.

"Junior!" Birdie said, again using that strange whispering shout.

"Junior!" Nola didn't bother with the whispering part.

The cabin door slowly opened. Junior emerged, smoothing his Mohawk. "Hey, guys," he said. "What's happenin'?"

"Junior!" Birdie said. "He's coming back!"

Junior nodded, like he was taking his time absorbing this information.

"Get off the boat, you moron," Nola said.

"Okeydokey artichokey." Junior swung himself over the rail and landed on the dock. Hadn't one of his flip-flops fallen into the drink when he'd gone on board? I thought so. So how come he now had flip-flops on both feet? One was black, like the flip-flop he'd lost. The other was red. Didn't someone I knew sometimes sport a pair of red flip-flops? I tried to remember who.

But there was no time for a real good remembering session, because things started happening fast. Junior said, "Loved when you asked him to show you the Harley, Nola. That was my favorite part, although—"

Birdie grabbed his hand and yanked him away from the boat, good and hard.

"Hey—where are we going?"

"Don't you realize what could have happened?" Nola said.

"Like, how do you mean?" said Junior.

"Zip it!" Nola grabbed Junior's other hand. They hauled him off the dock and into a clump of bushes, his feet hardly touching the ground.

Birdie glanced my way. "Bowser! Come!"

Did I have to? A snake had been in those bushes, and not too long ago. I'm not fond of snakes, especially the kinds with big heads and a certain sharp smell, a smell I was picking up now. But if Birdie says come, that's that. I trotted into the bushes.

The kids were hunkered down low to the ground,

peering through the leaves in an anxious sort of way—excepting Junior, who looked pretty relaxed—and talking in soft voices.

"I hate bushes like this," Nola said. "What if there's a snake?"

"It's spiky," said Junior. "Snakes hate spiky bushes."

"Huh?" said Nola.

I was with her on that.

"Well, don't you?" Junior went on. "I mean who would—"

"QUIET!" Birdie said.

We lay very still in the bushes. I listened hard for the steps of a very soft walker, and soon heard them. *Pat-pat, pat-pat.* Deke came padding along the dock, making no more noise than . . . a cat? Whoa! Was there something catlike about Deke? That couldn't be good. I watched him through a tiny space between the leaves. He was muttering to himself, mostly the kind of words Grammy never wants to hear from the mouth of any kid in her family, namely Birdie. Deke freed the line he'd tied to the cleat, boarded *Dixie Flyer*, cranked 'er up, and started chugging once more down the bayou.

"One thing I don't get," Junior said.

"Only one?" said Nola.

Junior continued on, like maybe he hadn't even heard her. "Why did he come back here?"

Birdie and Nola went into a long and complicated explanation, hard to follow even though I'd just been through the whole thing and therefore had the inside scoop. How crazy was that!

"Good job, team," said Junior. "I knew you'd think of something."

"We're not your team," Nola said.

"Just an expression."

"Never mind that," Birdie said. "Was there any sign of Snoozy in the cabin?"

"That's a strange question."

"What do you mean? It's the whole reason you went on board!"

Junior thought about that. "You may be right. But he wasn't there. And then the dude came back, and I jumped under the lower bunk—he's got bunk beds in there—and then we started moving and—"

"We know that!" Nola said. "Birdie asked if there was any sign of Snoozy—like he'd been in the cabin recently."

"Signs like . . . ?" Junior said.

"Something he left behind," Birdie said.

"Hmm," Junior said, followed by a few more hmms, and then, "Does Snoozy have a bathrobe?"

"Huh?"

"There was a bathrobe on a hook. It said 'Holiday Inn' on the front."

148

"How could that be Snoozy's?" Nola said.

Junior shrugged. "Maybe he stays at Holiday Inns."

"When Snoozy goes places, he stays with other LaChances," Birdie said.

"And would he wear a bathrobe to the tattoo parlor?" Nola said. "Think, Junior."

"I'm kind of too tired to think. It's been stressful."

"Stressful?" said Nola.

"Kidnap victim? Hello?" Birdie and Nola stared at him. "I was pretty brave, come to think of it," Junior added.

Not long after that, we parted ways with him, Junior headed for the food truck and us on our way to Claymore's General Store.

"Look at him," Nola said. "His flip-flops don't even match."

"Maybe it's a sign of genius," said Birdie.

Mrs. Claymore was on the porch, opening a big, brown cardboard box. And in that cardboard box were other smaller boxes, gold with a picture of a smiling member of my tribe on the front. I knew those gold boxes. There were biscuits inside and not just biscuits, but the crunchiest, tastiest biscuits around. I went closer to Mrs. Claymore, wagging my tail in the friendliest way.

She didn't seem to see me. Instead she looked up Nola and said, "Just had a most unpleasant call."

"Uh, who from?"

"That charter boat captain who bought the Weatherby. Claims we owe him a refund or some such nonsense. Two hundred dollars! What gets into the minds of some people?"

"I don't know, Mom," Nola said.

"Um," said Birdie, "what did you tell him?"

"What I tell every unhappy customer—as I'm sure your grammy does, too. He's welcome to return the purchase for the full amount, no questions asked. The gentleman didn't seem interested. He muttered something I didn't catch and hung up on me without a good-bye."

"Whew!" said Nola.

Mrs. Claymore's eyebrows rose. "Whew?" she said.

Birdie jumped in quickly. "She just means whew, like no harm done."

Mrs. Claymore gave Birdie a very close look, and then went back to unpacking the gold boxes.

"Let's go, Bowser," Birdie said.

Go? Now? This very moment?

"Bowser!"

"Actually," Birdie said as the two of us headed back to Gaux Family Fish and Bait, "Grammy only gives a full return if it's less than twenty-four hours and still in the original box."

As soon as she said "box" my mind zoomed right back

to the biscuits I hadn't had, and just when I'd gotten my mind to move on! Some days are easier than others.

We went inside. Grammy was alone, squinting at the label on a bottle of pills.

"Everything okay, Grammy?" Birdie said.

"Just fine." Grammy stuck the bottle in her pocket.

"Any news on Snoozy?"

"Nope. But are two days up yet?"

"No."

"What did I tell you about worrying?"

"Not to."

"We're good then," Grammy said. "Worrying takes it out of you. What you need are things that put it into you."

"Like what, Grammy?"

Was this important? I didn't know and I never found out, because at that moment the door opened. There'd been a lot of that lately, but were any actual paying customers coming in? Not that I remembered. How about this guy, tall and old, with thick white hair and an eagle nose? A paying customer or not? Maybe—whoa! An eagle nose? Hey! I knew this guy. It was Mr. Longstreet. Did we like him, me and Birdie? I kind of thought we didn't.

He walked into the store, glanced around, saw me and Birdie, and blinked in a confused sort of way. Then Grammy said, "Help you, sir?"

Mr. Longstreet turned his faded brown eyes on her. He

151

looked more closely—this was full-on staring, no doubt about it—and his face went from old and tired and crabby to something like wonder, one of best human expressions there is.

"Claire?" he said. "Claire Landry?"

"That was my maiden name," Grammy said. "Now it's Gaux. How do you—" She gazed at him. "Not Henry Longstreet?"

"The same," he said, and then he grinned a small grin, almost like a shy kid, and looked for second or two like a completely different person. "Well, not the same, of course. So much water under the bridge. Call it an ancient version of what was."

"Well, for heaven's sake," Grammy said. She held out her hand. Mr. Longstreet shook it, the kind of handshake where his other hand got involved, making a sort of sandwich of hers.

"Summer after freshman year in high school," he said.

"I remember."

"I ran away!"

"I remember that, too," Grammy said.

"That was how much I didn't want to leave."

Grammy shook her head at the memory of whatever they were talking about—at least that's how I understood that particular head shake.

"Like Romeo and Juliet!" Mr. Longstreet said.

Grammy's eyes shifted toward Birdie. Birdie's own eyes were open wider than I'd ever seen them. What was going on? I had no idea, although Mr. Longstreet was certainly right about lots of water going under the bridge—if he was talking about the Lucinda Street Bridge. I'd gazed down from the bridge many times—there happens to be a convenient lamppost halfway across—and watched that wide bayou flowing and flowing, never stopping day or night. It had to add up.

"I wouldn't go quite that far," Grammy said. She motioned Birdie in a little closer. "Henry, I'd like you to meet my granddaughter, Birdie Gaux."

"We've already met," said Mr. Longstreet, his old and crabby expression making a comeback.

12

H?" SAID GRAMMY.

Meanwhile, no hand-shaking was taking place between Birdie and Mr. Longstreet. Grammy turned to Birdie.

"When was this?"

"Yesterday," Birdie said. "When we went to pick up Snoozy."

"You and Lem?"

"And Bowser."

Yes, and Bowser! Had that somehow slipped Grammy's mind? No problem—I'm the forgiving kind.

". . . in Baie LaRouche," Birdie was saying. "We were on this beach and then Mr. Longstreet came up in a pirogue, and . . . and he had Snoozy's sunglasses."

"Snoozy's sunglasses?" said Grammy. "The sheriff told me they were in that stone hut on Little Flamingo Island."

"That's where I found them, Claire," Mr. Longstreet said. "Not knowing they belonged to this Snoozy character, of course. Up until last week I hadn't set foot in the state for more than half a century."

"Where have you been, Henry?" Grammy said.

"A long story," said Mr. Longstreet. He smiled at Grammy, his eyes brightening. "Which I'd love to regale you with. Anywhere nice I could take you for coffee?"

"Trixie's is all right," Grammy said. "Nothing fancy."

"Sounds perfect."

He extended his hand.

"Birdie?" Grammy said. "You'll watch the store? Won't be long."

"Uh, sure."

Grammy, moving kind of smoothly for her, almost light on her feet, approached Mr. Longstreet. He touched her shoulder. They walked together out of the store and into the parking lot.

Very slowly, like something was dragging her along, Birdie followed them as far as the door. I followed Birdie. Almost always I do my following from in front, but not this time for some reason.

We watched Grammy and Mr. Longstreet. They went to a pickup in the lot. He led her around to the passenger side and tried to open the door for her. Grammy waved him off and said something that made him laugh. She got in by herself. Mr. Longstreet climbed behind the wheel, not easily, backed the truck around, and drove off, headed up the bayou. A green pickup, by the way, with some buoys and nets in the back.

Birdie spoke softly. "Did you see that, Bowser? Mr.

Longstreet's ride is a green pickup. And with gear in the back."

I had seen that! I was in the loop! Did I feel good about it? The best!

"But what did Joe Don Matisse say? Moss green, maybe? Do you think that pickup's moss green?"

I couldn't help her with that, so I forgot about it immediately and went right back to what I'd been doing—namely feeling my very best.

Not long after that, Lem arrived, rubbing his hands together like he couldn't wait to get started.

"Take off, Birdie! I got this. Go on outside and be a kid."

"I am being a kid," Birdie said.

Pretty obvious. How could Lem have missed it? He didn't seem to care, just laughed to himself and picked up the phone. "Hey there, Lem LaChance down here at Gaux Family Fish and Bait. Got a quote on our Mardi Gras party cruise I was tellin' you about."

We went outside. "Mardi Gras party cruise, Bowser? We don't run a Mardi Gras party cruise. I wonder if Grammy knows."

I didn't have the answer to that one, but I had seen party cruises and I wanted no part of them. Meanwhile, we seemed to be on a nice walk, over to the central square with the stone soldier in the middle, and down the street that led to the little strip mall on the edge of town, just before farm country. Birdie opened the door to Joe Don Matisse's World Famous Tattoo Parlor and Spa and we went in.

No one was in the place except for Joe Don, bent over a sketchbook, his tongue sticking out the way human tongues do sometimes, and his pencil looking strange in his hand, almost like it was impossible for a hand so enormous even to hold on to a pencil without it slipping away. He looked up.

"Hey! Birdie. How ya doin'? Birdie and her faithful mutt—never did catch his name."

"Bowser. Mr. Matisse, I wanted to—"

"Nice," said Joe Don. "What kind of mutt is he, do you think?"

"The shelter lady said his ears are shepherdy, his tail's poodle-y, and his colors are like a Bernese. That's all I know."

"This was Adrienne?"

"The shelter lady? Yeah."

"Happen to notice her left ankle? That clown is my work."

"You tattooed a clown on Adrienne's ankle?"

"By request. I find clowns scary myself, but I don't argue with paying customers."

Or something like that. I was hung up on what I'd just heard about myself: shepherdy, poodle-y, Bernese-y. Wow! Sounded unbeatable. I wanted to hear more about that—much, much more. I searched my mind for ways to make the discussion go back there and came up with zip.

"So what can I do for you?" Joe Don said. "Let me guess—you want to learn the art of tattooing."

"Uh, no, sir. I actually came to ask you about moss green."

"Moss green?"

"Yes. You said Snoozy left in a truck that was moss green. I don't know what that is."

"Snoozy's not back yet?"

Birdie shook her head.

"Well, you know Snoozy," Joe Don said. "Doesn't run his life on anything you'd call a schedule." He opened a drawer full of nothing but pencils and selected a bunch, all of them green, to my way of thinking. "I'll take you through some greens, Birdie." He picked up a pencil. "This here is chartreuse green, really pops nicely on someone with very fair skin." He drew a bit of curve, picked up a different pencil. "Kelly green, useful for something of this nature." He tapped the snake tattoo on his shaved head, then drew some more on the paper, using pistachio, asparagus, viridian, olive, and other greens I didn't catch. Joe Don made his drawing with all of them, a drawing that, from my angle, seemed to be a human face. "And finally, moss green."

"Oh," Birdie said, "it's too dark."

"Too dark? I think it looks kind of nice, especially if I use it for the hair." He sketched in some hair above the human face, then held up the sketch for us to have a better look.

"Wow!" said Birdie.

I was with her on that. Joe Don had drawn a perfect picture of Birdie. It looked just like her, except for being all in green. He handed it to her.

"On the house."

"Thanks!" Birdie said.

We started toward the door.

"Birdie?"

We stopped and turned.

"Know why I asked if you were interested in the tattooers art?"

"No."

"Because you're the artistic type."

"I am?"

"Know how I know that?"

Birdie shook her head.

"Happen to have a brother-in-law—works over at WSBY, the Voice of Bayou Country. Program manager, in fact. And he played me a tape that come in on this contest they're running. A tape of you singing."

"There's three of us, actually—Nola Claymore, Junior Tebbets, and me."

"Uh-huh. Anyways, Roone—that's my brother-in-law—was impressed. I'm pretty sure he'd like to talk to you."

"Oh my god—are we going to win the contest? Junior will be out of—"

Joe Don made the stop sign. "Didn't say nothin' about the contest. This is more about Roone wanting to touch base with you."

"And the others? Nola and Junior?"

"Just you."

"So where are we, Bowser?"

We were on West Bank Road, which led from the Lucinda Street Bridge back to Gaux Family Fish and Bait. Birdie had to know that! We'd walked this way a zillion times, if zillion was a big number, and I was pretty sure it was. I gave her a close look. She didn't seem feverish or anything like that.

"Someone in a moss-green pickup drove Snoozy away from the tattoo parlor, but who? It wasn't Deke—he rides a Harley, doesn't even own a truck. And Mr. Longstreet's pickup is too light, actually more like kelly green. So who was driving that truck? Or am I being too fussy about the color? Maybe a cloud was covering the sun when Joe Don looked out, or maybe . . ."

Poor Birdie! I hated when she was worried. I leaned against her leg, cheering her up.

"Bowser!"

Did Birdie stumble? Maybe the slightest bit, but she didn't fall. Birdie has great balance, just one of the reasons we go together so well.

"What gets into you, Bowser?"

Did she seem more cheerful? I thought so. We went into the store. Grammy was by herself. Grammy by herself is always on the move—rearranging things, cleaning up, buying this, selling that, running the business. But now she was standing very still, gazing out the back window, a glass of ice tea in her hand.

"Hi, Grammy."

Grammy turned our way. She had a faraway look in her eyes. Had Grammy been daydreaming? If so, that was a first. She smiled a very warm smile, the kind where the eyes get involved. Coming from Grammy, it made me a bit uneasy.

"Hi, Birdie." She pointed with her chin. I love that human chin-pointing thing! "What you got there?"

"Oh," Birdie said. "It's this sketch." She handed it to Grammy.

"My, my," said Grammy. "This is very good. Who did it? Wait—signature right here at the bottom—J. D. Matisse, the 'J. D.' real small." She looked up. "Joe Don did this when we were there?"

"No," Birdie said. "Just now."

Grammy's dreamy-eyed look was fading fast. Fine with me: I prefer when humans stay put in their normal selves, if you get what I'm aiming at, and Grammy's normal self is far from dreamy. "What on earth were you doing over there?"

"Well, it's about greens, I guess. All the different shades of green. See how he used so many in the picture?"

Grammy examined it again, squinting this time. "Actually I didn't, but I do now. What got you interested in green?"

"I'm mainly interested in moss green," Birdie said. "Joe Don said the pickup that took Snoozy away from the tattoo parlor was moss green, so I wanted to make sure I knew exactly what that was."

"Why?"

"Because I saw a green pickup that might be the one—it even had some nets and buoys in the back, which matches up with what Mrs. Roux said."

Grammy shook her head. "I'm starting to regret telling you about Sherlock Holmes and his little clues. Didn't the sheriff say to give it a couple of days?"

"Yeah, but the sheriff—" Birdie stopped herself.

"What about him?"

"Just that he could be wrong, that's all. And anyway, it looks like the pickup I saw was kelly green, not moss green, except what if a cloud or something—"

"Kelly green?" Grammy said. "Where did you see this truck?"

"Uh, right here, Grammy. In our parking lot."

"You're talking about Henry's—about Mr. Longstreet's pickup?"

Birdie nodded.

"What a strange idea! You couldn't be suggesting he had something to do with Snoozy's disappearance—if he's even disappeared at all?"

Birdie didn't answer. She gazed over Grammy's shoulder, into the distance.

"Answer me, child." Grammy didn't say that angrily, or even especially loudly. She just spoke it plain.

Birdie turned her head slightly, now looking Grammy in the eye. "Mr. Longstreet hates the bounty hunters, Grammy. He said could strangle them with his bare hands. And he did have Snoozy's sunglasses."

"Which he found in that hut on Little Flamingo Island. But that's not even the point. Henry Longstreet could never kill Snoozy or anyone else."

"Because he's so old?"

Grammy didn't like the sound of that. "Are you being wise?"

"No, ma'am."

"Because age has nothing to do with it. I'm talking about morality. He's a moral person."

"But . . ."

"Out with it."

"But Mr. Longstreet talked about that, too. He said it's a lawman's job to stop lawbreakers but everybody's job to stop morality breakers."

"That doesn't mean killing them," Grammy said.

"I think he likes sharks better than people."

"That's nonsense. I knew Henry when he was just a little older than you. The time when you can really get to know someone. He's a caring person in general."

"Was he so . . . so fierce back then?"

Grammy's eyes got an inward look. "Now that you mention it, yes. But it was buried. His life and work brought it more to the surface."

"What did he do?"

"Well, I just found all this out, you understand."

"At Trixie's?"

"Exactly. We had so much catching up to do!" Grammy paused, coughed into her hand, that strange human cough where they don't really have to cough. Then why do they do it? Don't ask me. "After not seeing each other for so long, is what I'm trying to say," Grammy went on. "The Longstreets only lived here—meaning in Cleoma, where I grew up—for two years, eighth and ninth grade. His dad taught at the university in Lafayette, but he got a better job out west and they moved away. We lost track of each other. The distance was so much bigger in those days."

"It was?"

"Why, of course! You think all this social media of yours hasn't shrunk the country? Back then we had the US Mail, end of story, unless you could afford long-distance calls, which we could not."

"Did . . . did you miss him, Grammy?"

Grammy's eyes shifted. She took a deep breath. "Most likely not. It was a long time ago and we were very young, too young to go steady or anything like that."

"What do you mean, 'go steady'?"

"They don't say 'go steady' anymore? Good grief—figure it out. The point is, we lost track of each other. He ended up as a professor, like his father, got married—well, more than once, it seems—and now he's a widower and retired, involved with all sorts of environmental things. And I—well, I had the life I had, which you know about."

"It's not over," Birdie said.

Grammy gave her a long look and then a little nod.

"So," Grammy said, "let's have no more crazy talk."

"No more crazy talk," Birdie said. "But are you against the bounty now, too?"

"I am not."

"So it's all right to go after Mr. Nice Guy?"

"How many times do I have to say it? There's never been a bull shark in Betencourt Bridge."

"That's not what Mr. Longstreet says. He says his father took a photo of a bull shark all the way up in Montville."

"Isn't that interesting," Grammy said.

"Meaning you don't believe it?"

Grammy shook her head. "Meaning I might have to rethink a little."

"Grammy? Really?"

"Don't look so amazed."

13

BIRDIE SAT UP IN THE MIDDLE OF THE night. I always start off by sleeping on the floor beside her bed—which I think is what Grammy prefers, since she's mentioned it more than once—but I tend to climb up beside her somewhere along the way. Funny thing—I never remember doing it. I open my eyes in the morning and there I am, right beside Birdie! So I must be climbing in my sleep! Wow! But the point is that sleeping so close to Birdie, often with a paw on her shoulder in the friendliest way, I'm aware of how she's sleeping, which is usually very deep and very still. So when she suddenly sits up, I notice.

"Oh, Bowser, I just thought of something."

I wondered what it was, but not very much. The moon was shining through the window, turning Birdie into a beautiful silver statue, a statue with hair all over the place and one eye kind of puffy and almost closed. What a lovely sight!

"The turtle shell," she said.

I tried to concentrate. One thing I've found about concentrating: The harder you try, the harder it gets.

"Remember the turtle shell?"

Maybe. Sort of. Yes. No.

"Grammy said it got torn in two by a prop. But if Mr. Longstreet's right about bull sharks far up the bayou, then it was no prop and . . . and Mr. Nice Guy was in the swimming hole! In the swimming hole while we were swimming in it!" She drew up her legs. Both her eyes were wide open now, wide open and glowing in a silvery way that might have scared me if it had been someone else. I licked the side of her face, my only idea at the moment. She looked over at me, gave her head a quick little shake— I do the same thing myself—and lay back down. After not too long, she was back to sleep, although not the deep, still kind.

The next morning we were having breakfast—bacon and grits for Grammy, bacon and eggs for Birdie, kibble for me, plus a bacon tidbit or two Birdie slipped me on the side— when the sheriff stopped by.

"Good news," he said. "I heard from Snoozy last night."

"You did?" said Birdie.

"Well, not directly," the sheriff said. "He called in on the non-emergency line. After hours, so no one was there, but everything's recorded, of course." The sheriff took out his phone, tapped the screen a few times, laid it on the counter. Then came *buzz*, *buzz*, *buzz*, followed by Snoozy's voice. Hey! I missed him.

"Hello? Hey? Anybody home? This is Snoozy. Snoozy LaChance? From St. Roch? Hi there. The thing is—" Then came a muffled part, where—very, very faintly—I thought I heard Snoozy say, "Don't!" The muffling went away, and Snoozy spoke again, clearly, although maybe not as Snoozy-like as before, in a way that's hard to explain.

"I hear, um, people think I'm missing or something. Well, I'm not. I'm right here, doin' what I do. So don't worry 'bout me. Back just as soon as—" More muffling, and then: "As soon as I get done with this here project. Bye now." Click.

The sheriff rubbed his hands together, a human thing that comes after a job well done. "There we have it— Snoozy being Snoozy. Pretty clear to me that he's taking a little time off to go after that bounty. So I think we can all stop worrying—although I'm sure you'll have a word or two for him when he returns to work, ma'am."

Grammy thought that over and nodded.

Birdie said, "What was that muffled part?"

The sheriff shrugged. "Probably doing something else at the same time, had the phone between his shoulder and his ear and it slipped a bit."

"Can we hear it again?" Birdie said.

"Don't see why not," said the sheriff.

The sheriff played the phone call again. It was nice to hear Snoozy, but I stopped paying attention to whatever he was actually saying on account of an amazing discovery I'd just made: A piece of bacon had somehow gotten caught in the fur of one of my legs! I snapped that bacon up in no time. The day was off to a great start.

"I think I heard him say something during the muffled part," Birdie said.

"Yeah?" said the sheriff.

"Like maybe 'don't.'"

"I didn't catch that," the sheriff said. "Did you, Miz Gaux?"

"Nope," said Grammy.

"Can we listen again?" Birdie said. "Just one more time."

The sheriff laughed. "You're dogged, Birdie—I'll give you that."

Whoa! Had I ever heard anything so interesting? Birdie was dogged! It explained so much! I went right over and sat on her foot. Her hand came down and she petted my head, not the best petting like when she's really into it, more the distracted kind. But I'll take it! In fact, I couldn't have been happier: two dogged types against the world!

The sheriff replayed the call one more time. What was

all this about? Whether Snoozy was saying "don't" or not in the muffled part? Of course he was! How could anyone miss it? Also there was someone else in the background— no missing that, either, although whoever it was hadn't spoken, just kind of grunted in an unpleasant way.

"Don't hear it myself," the sheriff said.

"Me neither," said Grammy. "Do you, Birdie?"

"I'm not sure."

"And even if he did say it," the sheriff added, "I'm not seeing how it changes anything. Snoozy's a grown man behaving like some of our grown men behave in these parts. So let's just all relax."

"Agreed," said Grammy.

Birdie didn't answer. Maybe she would have, but then came a knock on the door. Birdie and I went to answer it.

A woman in a brown uniform stood outside, holding a big bouquet of flowers, tied with a ribbon. I heard the sheriff say, "I thought Birdie's mama was away."

"On a rig off Brazil," Grammy said.

Birdie read the card and brought the flowers inside. "They're for you, Grammy."

Grammy took the flowers, glanced at the card. The color of her face changed. I wouldn't call it blushing, exactly, but something close to it.

■　■　■

A hair-gelled dude in a red convertible was waiting for us at Gaux Family Fish and Bait when we got there to open up. Hair gel's something I can smell from a long way off. Humans add so many scents to their natural selves, for reasons I can't explain. Something I would never dream of doing myself, of course. The dude sprang out of the red convertible with a big smile on his face and strode over to us, a handsome dude in two-toned shoes of lovely soft leather, the nicest leather I'd ever seen. My mouth wanted very badly to get to know that two-toned leather.

"Hi, there," he said. "Mrs. Gaux, I believe? And this must be Birdie. I'm Roone K. Knight, program manager at WSBY, Voice of Bayou Country. Very pleased to make your personal acquaintance. I was wondering if—" Roone K. Knight stopped and looked down at his feet—where I happened to be, somewhat to my own surprise. "Heh, heh," said Roone. "This your pooch?"

"Yes," said Birdie.

"Very friendly," Roone said. "Seems to be licking my shoes."

Hey! He was right about that! Quick on the uptake and sporting quality footwear: Roone and I were going to get along great. Even the shoelaces—

"Bowser!"

What was that? Birdie calling me? Maybe not. Maybe I was just hearing things. That can happen to the best of—

"Bowser!!"

Yes, Birdie calling me for sure. Not the most convenient time, but when Birdie calls, I come. That's basic.

"Heh, heh," said Roone again. "Quite the character."

"One way of putting it," Grammy said. "What can we do for you, Mr. Knight? If this is about us advertising on your station, I can tell you off the top we don't do any advertising, period."

"No, no, nothing to do with that," Roone said. "Although our ad department is running a very nice promotion now until New Year's. But this visit is about Birdie."

"Birdie?" Grammy said. "I don't understand you."

"Well," said Roone, "you may or may not know about our song contest, featuring a five-thousand-dollar prize and a trip to meet a genuine Music City producer up in Nashville."

"I do not."

"Then maybe you don't know that Birdie sent in a song."

"I did not." Grammy turned to Birdie. When she turns like that, slow and deliberate, it's a kind of heads-up for trouble on the way, but not this time. Grammy's face softened and she said, "How come I didn't get to hear it? I like music!"

"I don't even have a copy, Grammy. Junior sent it in. The whole thing was his idea, and Nola pretty much wrote it. I just did a little bit of the singing."

"Modesty," Roone said. "A fine quality in a performer, and of course very marketable, goes without saying. But the fact is—well, before we get to that, Mrs. Gaux, I can actually play the song for you."

"That would be nice."

"Better yet, I can play it on the sound system in my car." We walked over to the red convertible, Roone leaned in, did this and that with buttons and switches, and then came the music, specifically those strange notes Nola had played on the guitar, not particularly loud but on Roone's sound system so rich and full, like mighty waves in the air.

"Wow!" Birdie said.

"Not state-of-the-art," Roone said. "But close."

The singing started up.

"Are you real, Mr. Nice Guy?

Mr. Nice Guy, Mr. Nice Guy,

Or are you a bad, bad dream?

Mr. Nice Guy, Mr. Nice Guy, Mr. Nice Guy."

We listened until the end. Roone shut off the player.

"It's about the shark?" Grammy said.

Birdie nodded.

"Mr. Nice Guy's a shark?" Roone said. "Like in more ways than one?"

"Huh?" said Birdie.

"Doesn't matter," Roone said. "What did you think, Mrs. Gaux?"

"I like it," Grammy said. "A lot."

"Really, Grammy?"

"I'm with you, Mrs. Gaux," Roone said. "It's a nice song. But that's not why I'm here."

"No?"

"No," Roone said. "Putting the song itself aside for a moment, what did you think of the singing?"

"It was good," Grammy said. "The way their voices went together."

"Uh-huh," Roone said. "Sure thing. But did any voice stick out from the others?"

"I don't like to say, being no expert. And also a blood relative."

"I respect that. And I'm not really an expert myself, although I did spend ten years managing bands out in LA. But an old Nashville buddy of mine is a genuine, gold-plated, top-ten-hit producer. I played him this little ditty and, long story short, he wants to meet Birdie."

Then all eyes were on Birdie. No surprise there. Who wouldn't want to watch Birdie? I do it pretty much all the time. She looked up at Roone. "This friend of yours—he wants to meet me and Nola and Junior?"

"Just you."

"Not the others?"

Roone shook his head.

"But it was Junior's idea. And Nola wrote almost the whole thing. I just sang a little."

"Lovely demeanor," Roone said. "Were you aware you've got perfect pitch, Birdie?"

"I don't even know what that is."

Roone laughed. "Marketable and in spades. Forget about perfect pitch. There's an unusual quality to your voice. Big—amazingly big, now that I see you in person—and honeyed at the same time. That's according to my buddy. So—any questions?"

"She's eleven years old," Grammy said.

"Going on twelve," said Birdie.

"Young singers aren't unknown in the music business, especially on the Nashville end," Roone said. "But all we're talking here is an introductory meeting—plus a trip to Nashville for you and your grammy with all the trimmings, on my buddy's company."

"Nashville," Birdie said.

"Correct," said Roone.

"Does this mean we're going to win the contest?"

"The contest?"

"Your contest—with our song about Mr. Nice Guy."

"Oh, that," said Roone. "The winner hasn't been

decided, but I can tell you we're down to three finalists and your song didn't make the cut." His eyes narrowed. "Is it the five K you're thinking about?"

"K?"

"The five grand. The prize. Because if my buddy's right and if things work out—no guarantees in this business—then five grand's going to be like chicken feed to you." Roone glanced at Grammy. "You and your family," he added.

Chicken feed? The first thing I'd understood in this whole conversation. I've tasted chicken feed. Not my favorite, but you can go way lower on the food chain, down to cigar butts, for example. So if Roone was promising chicken feed, it could have been worse. That was my takeaway.

Meanwhile, all eyes were back on Birdie. She was biting her lip and gazing down at her feet. Birdie was wearing sneaks today, nice blue sneaks with silver stars on them. The laces were silver, too, a sparkling silver that looked very pretty, although the laces on one shoe seemed kind of . . . chewed up? How would something like that happen?

"Could we—could Birdie have some time to think about this?" Grammy said.

"Sure thing," said Roone. "This is one of those cases where time is on our side. Not indefinitely—need to be realistic." He handed each of them a card. "My contact info. Get in touch anytime."

Roone jumped into his red convertible and zoomed off.

"What should I do?" Birdie said.

"What do you want to do?" said Grammy.

"I'm not sure. I don't—I don't even know how to . . . to . . ."

"To start thinking about this?"

Birdie nodded.

"Well," said Grammy, "suppose you'd made this record or whatever it is on your own."

"Without Nola and Junior?"

"Exactly. Then what would you say to this Roone character?"

Birdie closed her eyes. I could feel her thinking very hard, maybe harder than she'd ever thought. Was that how come she closed her eyes? I tried closing my own eyes. No thoughts came.

Her eyes opened. "I'd say yes."

"Well then," said Grammy.

"But I didn't do the song on my own."

"Right. But at least now you know what you'd want otherwise. Best thing now is to sleep on it."

Sleep? Now? It was still early morning. In fact, I could taste a few breakfast crumbs in my mouth, a pleasant discovery. But I didn't feel at all sleepy and Birdie looked pretty wide awake herself.

Birdie and I ended up going for a long walk instead. From time to time she'd say, "I just don't . . ." or "Should I tell Nola and Junior, or only Nola . . ." or "If I feel so bad about this, how can it be the right . . ." or other stuff like that. All I knew was that Birdie was unhappy. I tried to do something about that, namely by bringing her little gifts, like a nice rock, a fast-food wrapper, and even a dead bird I came upon under a bush in a scrubby patch at the edge of town.

"Oh, Bowser, put that down."

I laid the bird at her feet, expecting her to pick it up, admire it, possibly put it in her pocket. But she did none of those things. Instead, she looked around in a puzzled way, as though she didn't know where she was.

"Hey," she said. "There's Snoozy's place."

We went up to Snoozy's double-wide. Birdie knocked on the door.

"Snoozy? Snoozy? Are you there?"

No answer.

"What if he came back and he's sleeping so deep he can't hear me?" Birdie raised her voice. "Snoozy! Snoozy!"

No answer. Then a phone rang inside the double-wide. After a bunch of rings, I heard Snoozy's voice. "Hello,

hello, hello. This is the Snooze. Wait for the beep." There was some silence, followed by a click. So Snoozy was inside after all?

"I wonder," Birdie said. "I wonder about that message machine."

I waited to find out what sort of wondering she was doing, but Birdie didn't explain. Instead, she went over to Snoozy's pipe-smoking lawn gnome and took the key from the bowl of his pipe. Then she returned to the door, stuck the key in the lock, and turned it. Were we up to something new and fun? What a great idea! Birdie, the one and only.

14

WE ENTERED SNOOZY'S PLACE, STEP-
ping directly into the kitchen. It was
clean and tidy in Snoozy's kitchen, with
no dishes in the sink and the pots and pans hanging neatly
on the wall. Also on the wall hung lots of fish photos—fish
leaping, swimming, fighting on the ends of fishing lines.

"Snoozy?" Birdie said. "Are you here?"

I didn't think so. There was a hint of Mr. Manly smell
in the air, but not recent. We walked down a narrow hall,
looked into a living room with barely enough space for a
huge TV and a huge La-Z-Boy recliner, the most comfortable-
looking chair I'd ever seen.

"Bowser? What are you doing?"

No time to try out the La-Z-Boy now, not properly. I
trotted after Birdie. She was opening a door on the other
side of the hall. We looked into Snoozy's bedroom. The
bed, piled with many pillows, was made up. On the desk
lay a blue notebook, the kind Birdie sometimes brings
home from school. Birdie picked it up and read the writing
on the cover.

"'Secrets of Fishing, by Snoozy LaChance.'" She opened the notebook. "'Think like a fish. End of story.'" She turned the pages. "The rest is empty, Bowser. What does it mean?"

I had no idea. I was busy trying to think like a fish. No thoughts came at all. Was that the point? Wow! Snoozy turned out to be brilliant.

We went back to the kitchen. A phone sat on the counter. It had a small round screen on it, a screen that was flashing red. Birdie gave it a close look. "Ninety-seven new messages." She pressed a button. Then came a little bing and a woman said, "A fun Thanksgiving yesterday. Sorry you slept through the actual dinner, but everybody loved your crab cakes." *Bing.*

"Thanksgiving?" Birdie said. "But Thanksgiving's next month. He hasn't checked his messages in almost a year?"

We listened to more messages about this and that, lots of them asking how come Snoozy didn't return calls. "Why do I bother leaving messages?" was one. And "Wake up, moron!" was another.

"Let's just check the latest ones," Birdie said. She pressed the buttons.

Bing. A man with a very deep voice spoke. "Snooze. It's me. Heard about this bounty? Got a proposition for you. Meet me on the boat."

Bing.

"Hey, Snoozy LaChance? Name's Deke Waylon, down in Baie LaRouche. Run a boat called *Dixie Flyer.* Maybe you seen it around. Interested in making some legit green? Gimme a call."

Bing.

"Okay, Snooze, you win—fifty-fifty." It was the deep-voiced man again, the sound he made so rumbly it seemed to vibrate the walls. "I'll swing by tomorrow. Be ready—for once in your life."

Bing.

Nothing but a faint hum.

"That hum must be the call that came when we got here," Birdie said. "No message. But at least we have some clues. The next step is to deduce."

Deduce? Had I heard about that recently? Possibly and possibly not, like some other things in life. My guess? Deducing was not easy. I got no further than that.

Birdie opened the fridge. Did deducing have something to do with food? How interesting! We gazed into Snoozy's fridge, saw a box of doughnuts and a lemon. "There are two boat captains in this story, Bowser—two guys after the bounty. Deke Waylon was second. This other guy, with the deep voice, got to Snoozy first. And he's someone Snoozy knows. That's what I deduce."

Wow! Birdie had deduced all that just from one lemon and a box of doughnuts? Imagine if the fridge had been full!

She closed the fridge. "Is Snoozy all right? Or was there something fishy about that call of his?"

Call of Snoozy's?

"You know—on the sheriff's non-emergency line, when he said not to worry about him."

Oh, yeah! That one. As for the fishy part, anything involving Snoozy was fishy—let's not forget the fish tattoos on his arms, plus Mr. Nice Guy, or at least part of Mr. Nice Guy, on his chest.

"I think there was something fishy. But even if there wasn't, I have to know for sure. I hate not knowing."

Not knowing had never bothered me before, but if Birdie said not knowing was bothersome, then that was that. I got ready to start knowing things, and fast.

We went outside. Birdie made sure the door was locked. Then she put the key back in the gnome's pipe bowl and we headed for home. I had a brief moment to lift my leg within splashing distance of the gnome, satisfying for me but perhaps not worth mentioning.

Back at 19 Gentilly Lane, we'd barely gotten inside before the computer made a little ping. Birdie went to it, glanced at something blinking in one corner, tapped at the keys—and there on the screen was Mama's face. She called once a week or so, meaning once a week or so must have come around again.

"Hi, Mama!" Birdie said.

"Hi, sweetheart."

Mama looked tired, with dark circles under her eyes and a line or two on her forehead I didn't remember seeing before. In the background I could hear the rumble of some big machine at work.

"How are you?" Mama said.

"Good, Mama—and you?"

"Weather's been stormy but other than that no complaints."

"Is it dangerous?"

"Oh, no, nothing like that. This rig can take practically anything nature dishes out. But we've got some new crew members, so it's a bit of a learning curve for them."

"Meaning they get seasick?"

Mama laughed. "Constantly." Then her expression changed. "I had an email from Grammy."

"About Snoozy?"

"No. Why would you think that?"

Birdie started in on a whole long explanation about

Snoozy. I got lost pretty much from the get-go and just watched the changing expressions on Mama's face.

"Well," Mama said at last, "I think Grammy and the sheriff are probably right—it's just Snoozy being Snoozy. But this old boyfriend of Grammy's is interesting. I've never heard of him."

"I don't know if he was really a boyfriend," Birdie said, "but he sent her flowers yesterday."

"What was her reaction?"

"I think she kind of blushed, Mama."

Mama smiled. "That's nice," she said. Then she cleared her throat and the smile faded. "The email was actually about this song contest."

"Oh."

"Grammy says you have a tough decision to make."

"What should I do, Mama?"

"No one can tell you that," Mama said. "You have to do what feels right."

"What feels right," Birdie said, "is if this had never happened."

Mama laughed. "That's called turning back the clock. When you figure out how it's done, let me know."

Birdie looked away from the screen, eyes on nothing.

Mama stopped laughing. "Sorry, Birdie. I'm not

helping. It's just that talking to you makes me happy. I got carried away."

Birdie turned back to the screen. "That's okay," she said. Then she just looked at Mama. I had an amazing thought: Was Mama looking at her from wherever she was? Wow! I was understanding things like never before. It actually made me a bit uneasy, so I chewed my tail for a moment or two, got myself back to normal.

Mama took a deep breath. "Here goes, Birdie. Maybe this is bad parenting, but I'll tell you what I really think. There's a big stage in life, a big stage very few people get to play on. If you get a chance and you can do it without hurting people—at least not too much—then you should grab it. I know you're awfully young, but that's not so unusual in the music world."

"Am I really any good at singing?"

"I love your singing, although I'm no judge. But this Nashville producer *is* a judge, so why not hear what he has to say?"

"Because what about Nola and Junior?"

"This may sound harsh, but they'll get over it."

"And we'll still be friends afterward? Or not?"

"That's the big unknown."

Birdie bit her lip.

Mama spoke softly. "Want me to take a guess, Birdie?"

"Yeah."

"It will hardly affect Junior at all. Nola's a different story."

"How do you know?"

"Just a guess, like I said. And, of course, I'm not in a position to really know them, not like you."

"Because they're kids?"

"Partly. But I'm pretty sure Junior's the type who won't get knocked off track very easily."

"Junior's on a track?"

Mom nodded. "The big stage I mentioned? It's already on his radar. You getting a . . . what would you call it?"

"Nibble?"

"Exactly! You getting a nibble like this will only convince him he's not just dreaming."

"And Nola?"

"She'll be upset," Mama said. "Tempting to say that if it's a good friendship, it will survive, but that's just a kind of trickery."

"So there's no telling what will happen with Nola?"

"I'm afraid not."

In the background a man said, "Jen? We're up."

"Got to go." Mama blew Birdie a kiss. Not just to Birdie, of course, but to me, too. How nice of her!

188

■ ■ ■

We went into the kitchen. Birdie drank a limeade and gazed out the window.

Very softly she began to sing. No words—at least that I could pick out—but just sounds like *da-da-da-da-da-dah*. I found myself thinking of moonlight. And what was this? Moonlight seemed to shine from Birdie's eyes? I got the feeling she was far, far away, and I was happy when the singing stopped, even though it was so beautiful. Birdie being far, far away from me was out of the question.

Birdie took a deep breath and looked my way, her eyes clearing.

"Come on, Bowser. Let's try Junior first."

We left 19 Gentilly Lane and headed down toward the Lucinda Street Bridge. There was a single customer at Wally Tebbets's food truck, a big dude with black hair down to his shoulders and an earring in one ear. He kind of reminded me of a movie pirate we'd seen on TV, me and Birdie. On rainy nights we liked to watch movies. Watching movies means popcorn. I love popcorn. Popcorn has a way of falling to the floor.

Junior was down by the bayou, dangling his feet in the water and playing a harmonica. He saw us, played something real fast, and then said, "Hey!"

"You're learning the harmonica?" Birdie said.

"Just about got it perfected," Junior said. "And don't call it a harmonica."

"It's not a harmonica?"

"Of course it's a harmonica. But we call it a harp in the music business."

"Why?"

"Harmonica's not cool."

"But a harp's a kind of instrument you pluck, like in classical—"

Junior held up his hand. "I'm just saying how it's done in the music business, okay? So if you're ever in the music business you won't embarrass yourself."

From up in the food truck came Wally's voice. "One catfish po'boy with everything and a Red Bull. Anything else?"

"Um." Birdie gazed down at her feet. I myself heard a faint sound from out in the bayou, not quite a splash. I saw a little ripple on the surface, moving our way. Junior wiggled his toes, kind of small, like little white worms in the water. "Funny you should mention that," Birdie said, "because—"

At that moment came another voice from the food truck. "Nope, that'll do it." This was a very deep voice, maybe familiar to me.

190

Birdie whipped around and stared at the food truck. From where we were, we could only see its rear side. In the space underneath we had a view of the big pirate dude from the knees down. He wore sandals and had very wide, strong-looking feet with thick, round toes, so different from Junior's puny ones.

"Who's that?" Birdie said.

"Who are you talking about?" Junior said.

"The guy who just ordered from your dad."

"Yeah?"

"Do you know him?"

Junior gazed up at the food truck. "Don't recognize those feet."

Birdie started up the gentle slope toward the food truck. Junior rose and followed her. The ripple in the bayou, now close to the bank, subsided. I went after Birdie and Junior, soon got ahead of them, and reached the food truck first. The pirate dude was on the street, climbing into a pickup, possibly green in color, but I've heard I'm not at my best when it comes to colors. He fired up the engine and drove across the bridge.

Birdie and Junior arrived.

"Where'd he go?" Birdie said.

"Who?" said Junior.

"That customer." She glanced around. The pickup had

crossed the bridge and was making a turn. I barked and barked, trying to help.

"Bowser? What is it?"

I barked some more and Birdie finally looked in the right direction. Too late. The pickup was gone.

Birdie went up to the food truck counter. Wally was busy at the grill, his back to her.

"Mr. Tebbets?"

He turned. "Hey there, Birdie. What'll it be?"

"Nothing, thanks. But who was that customer?"

"The last one?" Wally scratched his forehead with the edge of his spatula.

"Yeah?"

"Don't know him—leastwise not his name. Been in once or twice. Always orders the catfish po'boy."

"Wouldn't mind one of those right now, Dad," Junior said. Then he saw a look on Wally's face and added, "If you're not too busy."

"Why in heck would I be too busy?" Wally said.

"Off the top of my head?" Junior said. "Can't think of any reason."

"Top of your head, huh?" Wally raised the spatula and smacked Junior right on top of the head. Actually not. It was a very slow swing and Junior had plenty of time to duck before scampering away.

"Care for a snack, Birdie?" Wally said. "On the house?"

"No, thanks, Mr. Tebbets," Birdie said. "But I was wondering if he paid with a credit card."

"Who?"

"That customer with the deep voice."

"Deep voice? Didn't notice that. But I don't take credit cards. Never have, never will. Cash, Birdie. Cash makes us free."

"It does?"

Wally nodded and was about to say something when he noticed Junior sitting in the grass, taking his harmonica apart with a screwdriver. Wally sighed. "What am I gonna do with him? Did you know he's got his heart set on making it in the music business? How come he can't be a sensible kid like you?"

"I'm really not," Birdie said.

"Tell me another one," said Wally.

We walked away, at first going at a steady clip in the direction of home. Then Birdie slowed down, almost came to a stop.

"This is so frustrating, Bowser. We know his voice. We know what he looks like. But we don't know his name. How are we going to find him?"

Hang around the food truck until he came back for another po'boy? That was my only idea.

"We could go back to Snoozy's and this time search through all the messages. Maybe the guy left more messages that might give us a clue."

I liked my idea better. My mind occupied itself with food-truck thoughts like po'boys, sausages, and bacon all the way to Snoozy's double-wide. Then I saw the gnome and decided that Birdie's idea was probably just as good as mine, possibly even better.

We went up to the gnome. Birdie fished around in the pipe bowl and went still. "It's not here."

She glanced at the double-wide. "Is Snoozy back? His car's not in the driveway."

We walked to the door. Birdie raised her hand to knock and then paused. "Would Snoozy use the gnome key?" she said, her voice low. "Or is it just for backup?" She put her finger across her lips. That meant we were being quiet. Always fun, especially for brief periods. Keeping real quiet, we walked around the double-wide to the back, hearing nothing from inside. There, parked next to a rusted washing machine, stood a green pickup with nets and buoys in the cargo bed.

Birdie's eyes widened. "Moss green," she said, very softly. She checked the double-wide again, still silent.

194

Then, on tiptoes, Birdie approached the pickup. Way up front in the cargo bed sat a big white cooler with writing on the side. "'Property of Snoozy LaChance,'" she whispered, and turned to me. "Stay right here, Bowser. Stay. In fact, sit."

I sat. Birdie scrambled up onto the cargo bed and made her way, sort of crouching, past all the fishing gear to the cooler. She was just about to open it when the back door of the double-wide opened and out came the deep-voiced dude with shoulder-length black hair. Birdie ducked down real quick, disappearing in the little space between the cooler and the rear of the cab.

The man strode to the pickup, almost not seeing me. But then he did.

"Huh? What're you doin' round my truck? G'wan! Get outta here."

But I couldn't, not with Birdie up there in the cargo bed.

"Don't listen good?" The man picked up a stone and threw it at me. The stone got me right in the shoulder and bounced off. A pretty hard throw, but it takes more than that to hurt ol' Bowser. Still, it got me real mad. When I'm real mad my teeth like to show themselves. I added in some growling, and all at once, there was nothing on my mind but charging this stone-throwing dude and showing him what's what.

"Last thing you'll ever do." He slid a gun out of his pocket. I'm no fan of guns, don't like the noise, for one thing. I hesitated. And in that moment of hesitation, the man hopped behind the wheel of the pickup and drove off, around to the front of the double-wide, down the driveway, and onto the road.

15

SOMETIMES IN THIS LIFE THE BODY TAKES over and you don't think. You just do. This was one of those times. Lucky for me, doing is what I do best.

For the next little while, my mind pretty much shut down, except for a kind of shouting it kept up inside my head. *Birdie! Birdie! Birdie!* Those shouts made me run even faster than I was already running, which was at top speed— meaning that now, for the first time in my life, I topped my top speed. That kind of over-the-top top speed makes your eyes water, your ears and tail stand straight back, and your paws hardly touch the ground. Was there something called the speed of light? I'd heard of it once or twice, a total mystery, but now I understood it completely. I ran at the speed of light, out around from the back of Snoozy's double-wide, across the driveway, and down the street.

Snoozy's street was the curving type, winding through the abandoned trailer park. I caught sight of the pickup through some trees and left the road, taking the beeline route. Don't get me started on bees, but the beeline was a brilliant invention on their part because in situations like I was in, it gets you where you want to go much sooner. Plus I was in a stinging mood myself, although knowing how to actually deliver a sting was something of a puzzle.

Birdie! Birdie! Birdie!

The pickup disappeared beyond a thick row of bushes, and when I saw it again it wasn't where it was supposed to be, but way off at an angle, raising a dust cloud. Had it turned onto a dirt road? I changed my beeline and started closing the gap. And crazily enough the gap seemed to be closing from the other end as well. How was that possible? Could the dirt road have been curving my way? Or was it something about the speed of light? I had no idea, just ran and ran and ran and—

And with no warning I suddenly burst through a thicket of sharp, spiky bushes and onto the dirt road! There, not far ahead, was the pickup, maybe slowing down a bit on account of all the potholes. Potholes don't bother me! I just kept running, heard some gasps, like maybe someone was fighting for air, poor guy, and closed that gap more and more.

Birdie! Birdie! Birdie!

There she was! I could see her head, raised slightly over the top of the big white cooler, a cooler belonging to Snoozy, if I had the details right, no guarantee. Birdie looked scared. How I hated to see that! And now the pickup began

198

to speed up. Why? Because all at once there were no pot-holes? We were on pavement? Oh, no! The gap was starting to grow. I was going to need more than all my strength. I'd never had to summon more than all my strength in my whole life, but now I did. *Bowser! More! More strength and right now this very second!*

And what do you know? It was there for me, more strength than I actually had! Birdie saw me, and she half rose behind the cooler. I dug in, running so hard that my claws dug up the pavement, sent chunks flying. I narrowed the gap again, got closer and closer, glimpsed the road widening and straightening up ahead, meaning this was my last chance, and launched myself in a tremendous leap, up, up, up—and onto the cargo bed of the pickup.

At that very moment, the deep-voiced dude—pirate, boat captain, whatever he was—hit the gas for real, and right away I found myself sliding backward, right off the edge of the truck and—

But no. Somehow I'd gotten myself caught in a tangle of fish net, which stretched and stretched and stopped my slide, leaving me hanging off the back of the truck, swinging this way and that, like . . . like some creature caught in a trap. I tried pawing, I tried squirming, I came close to trying panic—never a good idea, no matter what—and only got myself tangled more. Meanwhile, there was so much noise—the roar of the engine, the clatter of something loose under the truck body, the wind screaming past. I hardly heard the first grunt—and then another and another. That was Birdie's grunt! I knew every sound she made. Grunt, grunt, and slowly, one grunt at a time, Birdie hauled me back up onto the cargo bed.

There was time for one big hug—Birdie hugging me right through the net and making everything worthwhile, and then the truck made a sharp turn, hurling us right across the floor and wham against the side. Through the back window of the cab I saw the pirate glance in the rearview mirror, but he didn't see us, maybe because we were covered in nets and buoys and tarps and all sorts of gear.

We lay together, bouncing around and getting bashed by this and that. "Oh, Bowser, you're such a good boy." Which I knew, of course, but always nice to hear. I gave Birdie a lick through the netting and she gave me a pat in the same way. She spoke to me, almost in my ear. That tickled. I was so busy enjoying the tickling, I didn't really hear what she said. "We've got to get free of the netting, Bowser—that way we'll be ready to jump when he slows down." Or something like that. It was then I noticed how scared she was. The poor kid was shaking! Someone was going to be real sorry for that. I couldn't wait to find out who.

We got to work freeing ourselves from the netting, Birdie

using both hands and me using all my paws. You might think that I'd be better at work like that, but Birdie did not. She hissed in my ear. "Bowser! Stop! You're making it worse."

Me? How was that possible? Birdie must have been under stress. So my job was to help get rid of the stress, even if that meant doing something that made no sense. I lay absolutely still, apart for some panting that may have been going on, and let her take over.

I must have done a good job, because not long after that we were both free. Birdie crouched beside me, gave me the finger-across-the-lips signal, which meant . . . which meant . . . silence! That was it. I was so happy to have remembered I almost howled for joy, something I hadn't done in way too long. But this might not have been the moment. Instead we rose slightly, stuck our heads over the side of the cargo bed, and took a look-see.

Whoa! We were by the ocean? I hadn't been expecting that. Flat blue sea gleamed on and on in the sunshine, dotted here and there with low green islands and slow-moving fishing boats. On the land side lay one of those tree-filled swamps, with trees growing right out of the water. We had the road to ourselves, we meaning me and Birdie, which was always best, plus this pirate dude at the wheel, which was not so good. Was the plan to wait until he slowed down and then jump out? I thought so, but he was showing no sign of slowing down. I could see the back of his head and his thickly muscled shoulders through the narrow rear window of the cab. He was muttering to himself. I caught a few of the words, none of them the kinds of words you'd want to hear.

Staying very low, Birdie crept over to Snoozy's cooler, opened the lid just a little, and peeked in. Somehow I was already right beside her, helping her look. Always exciting to open something and see inside, but this was kind of disappointing. All Snoozy had in his cooler were cans of soda and some sandwiches in baggies—ham and cheese, salami and mustard, BLTs, all of which I knew from a single whiff. Birdie closed the lid, slow and careful, and—

"What the—" said the pirate up front. The truck swerved, slowed down, came to a stop. Birdie and I crouched behind the cooler. The cab door opened and closed. I heard the pirate climb out and start walking, but not around to the back of the truck, not in our direction. Instead, he seemed to be walking away.

We crawled over to the side, peered over. The pirate was headed toward a lone palm tree growing near the shore. Beyond the palm tree, a stone jetty extended out into the water. Tied up to a rusty post at the far end was a blue-and-white sport-fishing boat with a center tower and cabin in the bow. Small, yes, but very nice-looking.

202

"Bowser! What's *Bayou Girl* doing here?"

Bayou Girl! I thought I'd recognized it. Our very best boat. As for what it was doing here, that was easy: Someone must have driven it. There were only three people I'd ever seen at the wheel of *Bayou Girl*, namely Grammy, Snoozy, and Birdie, with supervision. So it had to be Grammy or Snoozy. Wow! Had I ever been this far out in front of anything?

The pirate reached the end of the jetty and yelled in his deep voice, "Hey! Anybody home? Hey!"

I heard no answer from inside *Bayou Girl*.

"Hey!" the pirate yelled again. "Snoozy, you—" He called Snoozy some names that won't be repeated here. The point was he sounded angry. Not at us. He'd completely missed the fact that me and Birdie were along for the ride, was totally unaware of us. That meant this was probably a good time to hop over the side and skedaddle. Or—and now I had an amazing thought—we could jump into the front and skedaddle in the pirate's own truck! I loved that idea. Did either of us know how to drive? Not me—I was perfectly aware of that, not being the type to get carried away by unrealistic notions, but how about Birdie? True, I'd never seen her drive a car. Did that mean she couldn't? Never rule Birdie out on anything. I gave her a close look. *Steal the truck, Birdie! Steal the truck!*

"Bowser—shh. What's wrong with you?"

Nothing. Nothing at all. As if that rumbling sort of pre-bark had anything to do with me!

"Bowser!"

I put a stop to it at once, whoever the culprit was.

Meanwhile, out on the jetty, the pirate was reaching for the bow rail of *Bayou Girl*. He grabbed it, pulled himself over and onto the deck, then walked around to the cabin door and disappeared inside.

"Is Snoozy in there?" Birdie said. "What's going on?"

I had no idea. Well, not entirely true. I did have one idea, involving a quick snack and Snoozy's sandwiches. Just sitting there in the cooler, at this very moment, doing no one any good. But possibly that wasn't the kind of answer Birdie had in mind.

She rose. "Come on, Bowser."

Meaning sandwiches were not in the picture, at least for now. Birdie stepped over the side and lowered herself to the ground. I jumped out and followed her—from in front, of course, Bowser style.

We walked to the shore, angling a little away from the jetty. At the water's edge, Birdie kicked off her shoes. "This has to be real silent, Bowser. We're going to swim out to the stern. Then we're going to climb up the ladder from the diving platform. After that . . . we'll . . . I'm not sure what we'll do. But don't forget—we have every right to be on

Bayou Girl. And nobody just ups and goes on board without permission."

What a plan! I'd never heard better.

We waded into the water, gently rippling water not as warm as in summertime but more refreshing, especially if you're like me, always in a fur coat. The water rose and rose and then I was swimming. That's the secret of the dog paddle—you just keep walking! Anyone can do it.

Birdie's a very good swimmer but not quite in my league because she hasn't advanced to the walking stage, still uses the crawl. I slowed down to not get too far in front, and soon actually had to speed up. What a good crawler she was! No one like Birdie, of course. We swam straight out to sea, as far as the end of the jetty, and then made a sharp turn, which took us right up to the stern of *Bayou Girl*.

Sometimes customers like to go snorkeling off the back of *Bayou Girl*, so we've got a platform that folds down to help them in and out. And more than a few of them need all the help they can get, believe me. You should see some of these characters! There's also a ladder bolted to the transom that helps them climb up. We paused by the ladder, just bobbing in the water. Birdie cocked her head to one side, meaning she was listening hard.

"I don't hear anything," she whispered. "Do you?"

I did, as a matter of fact. I heard a distant plane, a distant train whistle, and bubbles breaking on the surface somewhere farther out. Did any of that count? Probably not, because the next thing I knew, Birdie grabbed the lowest rung of the ladder—not the actual lowest one, which was underwater—and climbed the ladder with ease. She peeked over the transom, then unhooked the hooks that held up the dive platform and lowered it so it rested just over the water's surface. I scrambled up. We know our way around boats, me and Birdie. As for what we were actually doing at the moment, I had no clue.

Having no clue happens sometimes. Here's how I handle it: I do what Birdie does! It took me no time at all to figure that out. I had it in the bag from day one, meaning day one with Birdie. As for my life before Birdie, it wasn't very pleasant and doesn't bear thinking about—so I don't.

Right now Birdie was standing on the platform and peering into the boat. I rose up on my back legs and did the same, resting my front paws on top of the transom. No action on the deck of *Bayou Girl*. Some charts were spread out on the console and a thermos stood beside the engine control levers. Up front, the door of the cabin was closed and no sound came from inside. But I did hear a sound, namely a human footstep on the jetty. It was hard to see the jetty from where we were, on account of the bumpers hanging on the bow rail, so at first all we had were foot-step sounds. Then a man appeared, a tall old guy with an eagle nose: Mr. Longstreet.

He moved slowly and carefully along the jetty, binoculars hanging from his neck. Grasping *Bayou Girl*'s bow rail, he climbed over, not easily like the pirate, but in fact with a bit of a struggle, the binoculars swinging up and bopping that eagle nose. Mr. Longstreet muttered to himself, saying something that sounded to me like "clumsy old fool." On board, he went to the console—never once looking our way—took a key from his pocket, and stuck it in the ignition. He was just about to turn it when the cabin door opened.

The pirate stepped out. Mr. Longstreet saw him right away, his head snapping back as though he'd been hit.

"Who are you?" he said, his voice a bit quavery at first. He got it under control. "What are you doing on my boat?"

"Your boat? Got to do better than that if you're gonna lie to me. I know this boat and it sure ain't yours. Meaning you're a thief—a thief, as well as a kidnapper."

"Kidnapper?" said Mr. Longstreet. "You must be insane."

"Knock off the crap. I know who you are—the crazy old coot who likes sharks better than people."

"That's not true. But if we keep on—"

"Cut the crap," said the pirate. "All I want from you is Snoozy. Where is he?"

Birdie's eyes shifted to one side and she frowned, looking kind of confused. Why? Because we'd been thinking the pirate already had Snoozy? Wow! I was totally in the picture.

Meanwhile, Mr. Longstreet had raised his chin in one of those human looks that says *I'm better than you.* "I have no idea what you're talking about."

The pirate took a step forward. A big, strong dude: You could see it in every move he made. "There's some that fall offa boats in these parts and never get seen again. Get me?"

Mr. Longstreet nodded.

"So try another answer."

"Why should I?" Mr. Longstreet said. Kind of brave, but at the same time his legs were trembling. "I don't even know who you are."

The pirate took another step forward, his long black hair rising slightly behind him. "Name's Brock Stovall, number one charter boat captain in the western Gulf. I hired Snoozy to go after the bounty, as you know, and don't get me mad by denying it. I'm plenty mad already, and that's when bad things happen. You and everybody else around here knew that me and Snoozy were gonna find that bull shark first. No question about it—not with a team like that. Then the other night I left Snoozy at this camp we had and when I come back he's gone and there's signs of a struggle. You're maybe a weak old man, but Snoozy's no fighter." Pirate's eyes narrowed. "Or did you steal this boat and use it to try to lure him away? And he got suspicious and you clobbered him with . . ." Pirate glanced around, saw a boat hook near the bait box. ". . . with that there boat hook?"

"That's a complete fantasy," Mr. Longstreet said. "And I did not steal this boat. It was lent to me."

"You don't hear so good, do you?" said the pirate. "I told you no more crap and you keep up with the crap. This here craft belongs to Miz Gaux up in St. Roch, and she don't lend to nobody, not when it comes to boats."

Pirate took another step and this time didn't stop, but kept coming, real slow, muscles bunching with every movement.

Mr. Longstreet backed up. "All right, then, she didn't lend the boat. I chartered it. She charters boats."

The pirate smiled. Most human smiles are nice. This one was scary. "Sure, she does. Nice guess on your part. But what she wouldn't consider, no time, no how, is bare-boat charters. You can charter—and when you do, her or Snoozy is at the wheel." Pirate put up his hand like he was shading his eyes and peered around in an exaggerated way. Birdie pulled me down out of sight before I thought of doing it myself. Don't worry—it would have come to me.

Meanwhile, Pirate was saying, "But guess what. I ain't seein' them."

"This is ridiculous," Mr. Longstreet said.

We popped our heads back up, me and Birdie. Brock Stovall didn't like being called ridiculous—I could see it on his face.

"I've heard of this Snoozy character," Mr. Longstreet went on, "but I've never met him and have no desire to."

"See," Stovall said, "what's happenin' now is you're workin' your way around to the truth, but way too slow. Last chance. Where's Snoozy?"

"I have no idea."

"Did you kill him? Dump the body somewhere?"

"What a stupid thing to say!"

Stovall shook his head, like he was getting forced into something he didn't want to do. Then he started moving, the way humans do when their minds are made up. Mr. Longstreet backed away as far as he could before bumping into the console. He raised his big, bony fists like a trained boxer. Stovall knocked them away with the back of one hand. With his other hand, he grabbed Mr. Longstreet by the throat and lifted him clear off the deck. I felt Birdie gripping me tight by my collar, just helping me in case I was about to do what was in my mind. And I had been!

"Who's stupid now?" Stovall said, still holding Mr.

Longstreet in the air. Mr. Longstreet gurgled something. Then his eyes rolled up in his head and he went limp. Stovall gave him a disgusted look and dropped him on the deck. Mr. Longstreet's eyes fluttered open. He lay there, breathing heavily.

Stovall gazed down at him. The expression on his face changed, went from angry to sort of puzzled. He walked around to the front of the console, took the key from the ignition, and tossed it into the water. Then he hopped onto the jetty, untied the line, coiled it, and heaved the coil aboard, meaning we were tied up to nothing. He put the sole of his foot against the side of the boat and gave a big push. We drifted away from the jetty. A minute or two later I heard him starting up the moss-green pickup and driving off.

16

BIRDIE STEPPED OFF THE PLATFORM ONTO the ladder and scrambled up. I did the same. That might be a bit of a surprise, but I can climb ladders—at least this one. Birdie taught me on the very first trip I took on *Bayou Girl*. The customers always like seeing me zip up the ladder, and often try giving Birdie a tip. Birdie is not allowed to accept tips, as Grammy has made clear in no uncertain terms. Plus there are a lot of other rules the customers have to follow. We run a tight ship at Gaux Family Fish and Bait, meaning no nonsense. But if you ever come out with us on *Bayou Girl*, remember that there's nothing nonsensical about slipping a treat to any ladder-climbing four-footed types who happen to be on board. Meet me on the dock after the trip's over and Grammy's back in the shop.

We stepped down onto the deck. Mr. Longstreet was sitting up, his back against the console, looking very pale. He saw us and frowned in a confused way, even closed his eyes and reopened them, like he was seeing if we were real. Ha!

"Are you all right, Mr. Longstreet?" Birdie said.

He nodded a weak sort of nod.

"Don't move." Birdie hurried to the bow. She opened a locker, dragged out the anchor, a big, heavy thing with a curved, two-pointed bar at the end. Birdie tied the end of the anchor line to the bow cleat, and then squatted down and with a loud grunt lifted the anchor and heaved it over the side. Anchor line ran out, disappearing beneath the water. *Bayou Girl* gave the tiniest lurch, stopped drifting, and lay still.

By that time Birdie was already fishing around again in the locker. Out came what all the waterfront people in St. Roch called "Miz Gaux's Invention for Finding Stuff Dumbasses Lose at Sea," or just "Miz Gaux's Invention" for short: a bright orange buoy tied with a short length of line to a barbell. Birdie hauled it to the side of the boat where Stovall had stood when he threw the key overboard. She pointed to a stretch of water to our rear. "We must have been somewhere around there, Bowser."

I'm sure she was right about that, whatever it was. With another grunt, she swung Miz Gaux's Invention over the side in the direction she'd pointed out, but it didn't go very far, on account of the barbell being so heavy.

"Have to do," Birdie said, already putting on her gear—mask, fins, and snorkel. She glanced at Mr. Longstreet, still sitting up, although his eyes were closed. "You stay here with Mr. Longstreet, Bowser. Got that? Sit!"

I sat, no problem. What was hard to get about that?

Birdie sat backward on the gunwale, tipped over, and splashed down. She swam off toward the bright orange buoy, moving very fast, as she always did with fins on. Then she slowed down and started circling, her face in the water. I could feel how hard she was concentrating even from where I was, back in the boat. Imagine how strongly I'd be feeling it if I was out there with her! I checked Mr. Longstreet. Still breathing, at least a little bit, and therefore nothing to worry about, as I'm sure Birdie would have agreed.

The next thing I knew, I was going for a nice swim in lovely, refreshing water. How had I gotten here? No idea, but once I was in, why not paddle my way over toward Birdie? I couldn't think of one single reason.

Birdie had moved on past the buoy when I reached her. She was still swimming in slow circles, gazing down at the bottom, a sandy bottom with only a little seaweed here and there. For some reason, she didn't seem to notice me, even though I was right there beside her. To help her out, I pawed at one of her fins.

Wow! Birdie almost jumped clear out of the water! That had to be because she was so happy to see me. She pulled

214

off her mask and . . . and actually did not look that happy after all. "Bowser! Didn't I tell you to stay on the boat?"

I did my very best to remember, came up with not much, one way or the other.

"Oh, Bowser. What am I going to do with you?"

That was an easy one. Take me for long walks, give me lots of treats, play fetch—and those were right off the top of my head.

"All right. Just stay here. Don't go away. Don't do anything."

Perfect. I stayed there with Birdie and didn't do anything but paddle a bit. Birdie went back to circling slowly around. Then she was still. I heard her taking deep breaths through the snorkel. She jackknifed down in the water, her fins slipping through the surface with hardly a sound. Down, down she went. At the bottom—not too deep, not like her dive at the swimming hole where she'd found the turtle shell—she reached out and grabbed something shiny.

Birdie swam her way up to the surface, those skinny legs kicking so smoothly, and held up the key. "Back in business," she said, or something like that: hard to hear her clearly with the snorkel in her mouth. We swam back to the dive platform. As I climbed on I was aware of some sort of shadowy form not far from the bow end, but you get all kinds of shadowy forms at sea, and often they're just clouds passing over the sun. You learn stuff like that in the charter boat industry.

Mr. Longstreet was standing up when we got back on deck. His gaze went to Birdie, to me, and then to the key in her hand. He blinked once or twice.

"Birdie?" Mr. Longstreet's voice was weak and whispery. "I wouldn't mind some water."

Birdie nodded and went into the cabin. She brought back a bottle of water and gave it to him. Mr. Longstreet tilted it up to his mouth and drank. Color started returning to his face right away, and when he spoke again his voice was almost back to its normal self.

"Thank you, Birdie. But—but what are you doing here?"

Birdie tilted up her chin. Hey! I started to notice that maybe Birdie wasn't acting her friendliest with Mr. Longstreet. "What are *you* doing here, Mr. Longstreet? How come you've got *Bayou Girl*?"

"Claire—I mean, your grandmother—lent it to me."

"Lent?"

"Well, I offered to pay the normal charter price. Insisted, in fact. But she wouldn't hear of it. I plan to treat her to a nice dinner instead."

"She let you take it by yourself?"

Mr. Longstreet made an effort to stand taller. "I grew up around boats, as she knows very well. I've sailed around the world."

"Grammy doesn't let anybody drive this boat except her and Snoozy."

"She made an exception in my case."

"Why?"

"You'll have to ask her." Her glanced around. "Is she with you?"

"With me?"

"We're miles from home—your home, I mean. How did you get here, if not with her?"

"I—I got a ride with someone else."

"But how did you know I was here?"

"I didn't. I saw the boat."

Mr. Longstreet blinked again. "Did . . . did you see anyone else on the boat?"

Birdie gazed up at Mr. Longstreet, a very steady gaze that made me proud of her. Yes, he was old, but a grown man, and Birdie was just a kid. "Did you do something to Snoozy?" she said.

His face reddened, but in patches, not all over. "Does your grandmother know what an impertinent child you are?"

"She knows me," Birdie said. "And another thing— Snoozy means a lot to her. Did you do something to him?"

"What are you accusing me of?"

"You said you wanted to strangle the bounty hunters with your bare hands. And Snoozy went off on the bounty hunt. You had his sunglasses."

"I explained all that. What I said was just an expression."

"'Strangling with your bare hands' was just an expression?"

"I don't like your tone, not one little bit." He started wagging his finger at her. Why is finger wagging such an unpleasant sight and tail wagging such a delight? I didn't know. I tried to imagine Mr. Longstreet wagging his tail, but could not. "Where do you get off, thinking you can interrogate me like I'm some crimin—" Mr. Longstreet started coughing—deep, painful-sounding coughs that doubled him over. He staggered, felt around for a handhold, found none, and sagged against the side of the boat.

"Mr. Longstreet? What's wrong?"

He kept coughing but at the same time waved Birdie away angrily. Birdie turned out to not get waved away so easily. She stepped forward, put her hand on his back, and guided him over to one of the bench seats. Around then was when I noticed that the water bottle had fallen on the deck. I picked it up, went over, and waited for Birdie to notice. At first she didn't, so I pressed against her, which is our go-to method in situations like that.

"Good boy," she said, holding the bottle up to Mr. Longstreet's mouth. Meaning the good boy was me, not Mr. Longstreet. I don't want any confusion about that.

Mr. Longstreet, his face gray and waxy, took the bottle and sipped some water. A trickle ran down his chin.

"Are you all right?" Birdie said.

"Just . . . just . . ." With his free hand, he tried to reach inside his shirt pocket, but couldn't quite do it, his fingers trembling the way they were. Birdie reached in for him, withdrew a small white pill. She held it out. He tried to take it, but his hand was too unsteady.

"You'll have to . . . to do it for me," Mr. Longstreet said.

"Do what?"

"Stick it under my tongue."

I could see on Birdie's face that she didn't like that idea, not one little bit. Mr. Longstreet opened his mouth and raised his tongue. Birdie placed the small white pill under it. Mr. Longstreet closed his mouth, which was fine with me. He had one of those mouths that looked much better closed than open.

"Should we go to the hospital?" Birdie said.

Mr. Longstreet shook his head. He sat very still, like he was concentrating on something. Maybe the pill under his tongue? That was my only thought. Meanwhile, his face was looking less gray and waxy. He took a deep breath.

"That's better," he said. "No hospital. I'm fine now. And . . ." He gave Birdie a little smile. "And thank you."

Birdie did not smile back. "You can say thanks by telling me what happened on Little Flamingo Island."

Mr. Longstreet's smile faded fast. "I don't know what you mean."

"Something happened to Snoozy out there and I think you know."

"If something happened I know nothing about it," Mr. Longstreet said.

Birdie stepped away from him, looked out to sea. "Why do you have *Bayou Girl*?"

"I already explained. Your grandmother—"

"But where were you going? Is this a fishing trip?"

"The reverse," Mr. Longstreet said.

"I don't understand."

Mr. Longstreet rose. "I can show you." He approached the console, a bit unsteady.

"Better sit down," Birdie said. "I'll drive."

"You're old enough to drive this boat?"

"Yes."

"I mean according to the regulations."

"I have a license."

"A license for a boat this size?"

"A license," Birdie said.

Mr. Longstreet seemed to be thinking. "When I was a boy here we kids operated boats all the time and no one thought anything of it. But I would have expected things were different now."

Birdie nodded like that made sense, at the same time saying nothing. Then she went to the other side of the boat and hauled in Miz Gaux's Invention, stowed it away. After that, she stuck the key in the ignition, fired up the inboards, walked to the bow, raised the anchor, coiled the anchor line, returned to the console, and hit the throttles. *Bayou Girl* got under way, moving in a slow, easy curve. Birdie turned to Mr. Longstreet, who'd been watching her the whole time. "Where to?" she said.

Mr. Longstreet gazed over the water and pointed. "Eleven o'clock." He sat back down on the bench.

Ah! The open sea! There's really nothing like the open sea, and we don't get out on it nearly enough, most of our work, mine and Birdie's, being on the swamp tours or fishing charters on the lakes and bayous. I love the swamps, the lakes, and the bayous, but there's no denying their smell, which is all about rot. Out on the open sea, the air is like nowhere else, fresh and salty and . . . alive! Yes, alive! I gave myself a wonderful shake, so tremendous I actually felt things rattling around in my head. Birdie maxed out the throttles and the bow rose up as *Bayou Girl* felt the power of those engines. Mr. Longstreet practically slid off the bench seat, held on with what I believe they call a death grip. You can't have more fun than this.

The waves picked up the farther we got from shore. That meant we started bouncing around a little. Round about now was when a customer or two might start feeling pukey. Not me and Birdie, of course: We were natural-born sailors. Was Mr. Longstreet feeling pukey? I wasn't sure. He sat on the bench, eyes out to sea where some boats clustered together, black against the horizon. Was he even a customer? I wasn't sure about that, either.

As we got closer to the boats, Mr. Longstreet rose and made his way, hunched over and with careful short steps, over to Birdie. Birdie at the wheel: What a lovely sight! Somehow her body absorbed all the bumps handed out by the waves in a nice, easy rhythm, almost like she herself was part of the sea. Mr. Longstreet was not part of the sea. He held tight to the console and came close to losing his balance once or twice.

"Slow down," he said. "Please."

Birdie backed off the throttles, and *Bayou Girl* rose— Birdie rising, too, on her tiptoes, to see over the bow—and settled down.

"Was it too bumpy for you, Mr. Longstreet?"

He shook his head. "I want to go in slow, that's all."

"Go in where?" Birdie said.

Mr. Longstreet pointed toward the boats, much closer now, all of them around *Bayou Girl*'s size, or bigger. I spotted people on the decks now, and up on the tuna tower of the nearest boat, a man with a rifle.

"Do you see what they're doing?" Mr. Longstreet said.

"No."

He stabbed his finger at one of the charts clipped to the console. "Those boats are sitting right there, on the deep side of Sawtooth Reef. Know why?"

Birdie shook her head.

"Because sharks hang out in these waters, especially this time of year. Might be on account of the water temperature, maybe a seasonal change of the currents."

On one of the boats, a man dumped a bucket over the side.

"Oh, those, those—" Mr. Longstreet cried out. "Do you see what they're doing?"

"Chumming?"

"Savages!"

"But isn't it legal?"

"So? Does that mean it should be? Throwing blood and guts into the natural habitat to lure harmless predators living out their lives as nature intended?"

"Harmless predators?" Birdie said.

Mr. Longstreet gave her a sidelong look. "Children used to respect their elders."

He waited for Birdie to reply, and when she did not,

he said, "Slow down a bit more and then head right through them."

"Right through those boats?"

"Not hitting them," Mr. Longstreet said. "Just making a statement."

"I don't think that's a good idea. Grammy always says to be extra careful around other boats."

Mr. Longstreet's mouth opened and I got the feeling angry words were on the way, but instead he paused. "She—she's correct, of course. A very smart person, then and now. But there are special cases in life and—"

The nearest boat was close enough now for me to make out the gold chain glistening around the neck of the man in the tuna tower. He went still, aimed his rifle at something that thrashed just under the water, and then came the crack of a gunshot.

Another man on board reached over the side with a gaff, its barb flashing in the sunshine, and hauled in a shark, about his own size and no longer moving, just hanging limp on the hook.

Mr. Longstreet shouted in fury and shook his fist in the air. No one on the boats seemed to notice him. He screamed at them, "You're going to pay!" Then he reached past Birdie and shoved the throttles down to the max.

17

I WENT SKIDDING BACKWARD ON THE DECK.
Birdie might have, too, except she was hanging on to
the wheel. Her feet slid out from under her, and for
an instant or two she was stretched straight out in the air,
like she was flying. Up ahead, the circle of boats seemed
to be racing our way with amazing speed, even though we
were the ones on the move. Birdie got her feet back down
on the deck, turned the wheel hard with one hand, and
reached for the throttles with the other.

"Don't you dare!" Mr. Longstreet shouted. And then he
did something terrible: Mr. Longstreet laid both his hands
on Birdie's shoulder and gave her a push. Not just a little
push, but a real strong one, especially for someone so old
and sick. Oh, yes, he was sick—I'm good at smelling sick-
ness in people. But that didn't matter now. All that
mattered was what he had done to Birdie, now sitting on
the deck and rubbing her arm, a stunned look on her face.
Mr. Longstreet grabbed the wheel and steered us straight
for the nearest boat, the one with the rifleman in the tuna
tower. The rifleman was shouting something that I couldn't

make out over the roar of *Bayou Girl*'s engines. And the men on other boats were shouting, too, and waving their arms and hurrying this way and that. Meanwhile, Mr. Longstreet was hunched over the wheel, gripping it so tight I could see his knucklebones through the skin.

No one pushes Birdie around. That was basic. Rule number one. A ferocious growling started up on the deck of *Bayou Girl*, the kind of growling that means big-time action is on the way, and pronto. I charged, charged at full speed, holding nothing back. Holding things back is not my strong point in general, but it's extra true for when I'm on the attack.

Here's another thing about me on the attack: My memories of what actually happens are always kind of confused. For example, I'm pretty sure that I barreled into the backs of Mr. Longstreet's legs and right away came an "Oof!" that was part grunt and part a cry of pain, totally satisfying to my ear. But after that, did he lose his grip on the wheel? That would be my guess. I have sort of an image of him in my head, stumbling away from the console. Did he also lose his balance and start to fall over the side? Was Birdie back on her feet and somehow there at the very last second, just in time to grab his sleeve and pull him back on the boat? And were we meanwhile almost right on top of the boat with the rifleman in the tuna tower? Was there lots of bellowing and screaming mixed in with the roar of engines, and not only *Bayou Girl*'s? In short, were we headed for disaster? I can't help you with any of that.

But here's one clear memory: Birdie! Specifically, Birdie racing to the console, yanking back the throttles, jerking the wheel hard to one side. I saw that for sure! The look on her face? Calm! I'll never forget it. *Bayou Girl* tilted way over and we carved a very sharp turn in the water, driving a big curling wave toward that nearest boat. It rose up high on the wave, almost right above us. The rifleman's eyes and mouth were wide open. He grabbed a rail, at the same time losing hold of the rifle, which spun down into the sea and vanished. I have a very strong memory of that part, too, meaning the disappearance of the rifle: an interesting sight, even strangely beautiful.

We sped away from the bounty-hunting boats, headed back toward land. Was the excitement over? I missed it already, but maybe that's just me. I trotted over to Birdie, at the wheel. Without taking her eyes off the sea, she gave me a pat.

"You're the best," she said.

Tell me something I don't know! But it was nice to hear it from Birdie. I was about to lick her feet, just letting her know I was thinking of her, when thumping sounds came from behind me. I twisted around and saw that my tail was thumping against the console with every second wag, if that makes any sense. Probably not. I also noticed Mr. Longstreet slumped half on and half off the padded bench seat. He had a cut on his forehead, not bleeding much, and his face was waxy again. Our eyes met. His were not friendly. My choices were to bite him good and hard or look away. I opted for looking away, but it was close.

By then we were close to land. Birdie pointed out a familiar building on shore, shaped like a gigantic milk shake.

"Shakey's Shakes," she said. "The mouth of the bayou's just beyond the next point. We'll be home in—"

Sirens! Sirens so high pitched my ears could hardly stand it. Out from behind the point that led to the bayou zoomed a black speedboat with gold trim, four big outboards mounted in the stern, blue light flashing in the bow.

"Oh, no, water patrol," Birdie said, throttling back. "Maybe it's not us."

But it was us. A huge man stood up in the bow of the speedboat and spoke through a bullhorn. "Heave to!"

Birdie throttled back all the way. The sirens died down. We bobbed gently on the water. The patrol boat drew alongside. I didn't know the driver, but the huge man with the bullhorn was familiar: Officer Perkins, my favorite of all Sheriff Cannon's people, on account of biscuits he carried in his back pocket, day and night. I considered him a pal, and I knew he thought the same about me.

"Is that you, Birdie?" said Officer Perkins in his rumbly voice, the bullhorn now at his side.

"Yes, sir."

He looked into our boat, saw Mr. Longstreet slumped on the bench seat.

"What's going on, Birdie? What are you doing here?"

"Um," said Birdie, "it's a sort of charter."

"With you driving?" said Officer Perkins. "You know you're too young to operate a vessel of this size. And I can't believe your grandmother would ever allow it, certainly not without her beside you. Is she on board?"

"No, sir."

"But she approved this charter anyway?"

"I think so."

"You think so?" said Officer Perkins. "Not tryin' to be funny with me now, are you, Birdie?"

"No, sir."

"Because we got some very unfunny calls from vessels out off Sawtooth Reef concerning dangerous operation of this here boat."

"I know," Birdie said.

"You know about the calls?"

"No, sir. I meant the dangerous operation."

"You don't deny it?"

Birdie shook her head.

Officer Perkins's gaze moved on from Birdie to Mr. Longstreet on the bench seat, the bleeding from his forehead pretty much stopped, and back to Birdie.

"Who was at the wheel?" said Officer Perkins.

"When you pulled us over?" Birdie said. "Me."

"You know I don't mean that," said Officer Perkins. "Why take the blame for something you didn't do? Can't hardly think of a circumstance where that makes sense, and this one sure don't. I'm asking who was at the wheel when the dangerous part was going down."

Birdie thought for a moment or two, always nice to see. She's the best thinker I know. For example, who thought of adopting me from the shelter? Has there ever been a better idea than that?

She nodded her head, just a tiny nod that meant things were all straightened out in there. "It was Mr. Longstreet."

Mr. Longstreet looked up. "And I don't regret it—not one single bit."

Officer Perkins took out a notebook and wrote in it. He spoke as he wrote, the way humans sometimes do. "'Don't regret it—not one single bit.'" He stuck the notebook back in his pocket, then motioned to the officer at the helm of the patrol boat, who steered closer to *Bayou Girl*, almost touching. "Law says I can board in these type situations, Birdie." He stepped across the narrow opening between the boats and onto the deck of *Bayou Girl*. The patrol boat driver tossed him a line.

"What are you doing?" Birdie said.

"Towing you into the dock in Baie LaRouche."

"Towing?" Poor Birdie: She looked so unhappy at that moment.

"Towing. You're too young and this old gentleman is too dangerous. I could impound the boat, Birdie. Understand?"

"Oh, Officer Perkins, please don't do that. I—"

He held up his hand. "But I ain't gonna," he said. "Instead, I'm calling your grandmother, have her come down and collect the vessel."

"Uh, is there maybe some other way?"

"Yeah—towing, like I said."

"I meant some other way that leaves Grammy—that doesn't involve her."

Officer Perkins gave her a close look. "Birdie? Did your grandmother know you were on the boat?"

Birdie shook her head.

"Does that mean you didn't board her up in St. Roch?"

"No, I didn't."

"Then where did you get on?"

"It's kind of a long story."

"Tow job like this is slow going," Officer Perkins said. "Gives us plenty of time to hear even real long stories on the way in."

He tied the patrol boat line to *Bayou Girl*'s bow cleat, and soon we were on our way—*Bayou Girl* not under her own power, just sort of wallowing along in the wake of the patrol boat. Officer Perkins took Mr. Longstreet into the cabin and had him lie down. Coming back on deck, he said, "Okay—I'm all ears."

Oh, really? Not to my way of thinking. In fact, for a dude his size, his ears were on the small side. They probably didn't even work very well. I felt a bit sorry for Officer Perkins and spent most of the trip into Baie LaRouche keeping close watch on his ears. Meanwhile, Birdie launched into a story about leaping onto a moss-green pickup, and Brock Stovall, the pirate dude, and Snoozy, and a camp on Little Flamingo Island, and lots of other stuff, all of it kind of familiar but at the same time impossible to keep up with. All I really learned was that wallowing makes you sleepy.

The water patrol had a building at one end of the Baie LaRouche dock. There was an office in the back, away from the water, and that's where we all sat—Sheriff Cannon and Officer Perkins at one end of the table, and Grammy, Birdie, and me at the other. Mr. Longstreet sat by himself on one side.

"Drove *Bayou Girl* straight at those boats?" Grammy was saying.

"At full speed," said the sheriff. "We have multiple reports. And there was nothing accidental about it. Officer Perkins, will you read for Miz Gaux what Mr. Longstreet said regarding his actions?"

Perkins took out his notebook and read aloud in his rumbly voice: "'Don't regret it—not one single bit.'"

The sheriff turned to Mr. Longstreet. A bandage now covered his forehead cut and there was more life in that eagle face. "Do you deny making that statement?"

"No," said Mr. Longstreet.

"Do you deny the dangerous operation of *Bayou Girl*?"

"I do not."

"Henry," Grammy said. "Look at me and say that again."

Mr. Longstreet turned to her and held her gaze. "I'm sorry, Claire. My intention was only to observe and maybe try to reason with those bounty hunters. But when I saw what was going on I'm afraid I lost my head."

Losing your head would make anyone afraid, of course, so my inclination was to cut Mr. Longstreet a little slack.

Just one problem—there was his head, still attached to his neck like always. Right then, I stopped trusting Mr. Longstreet for good.

"Does that happen to you a lot?" the sheriff said. "Losing your head?"

Whoa! Did the sheriff not notice Mr. Longstreet's head sitting there in its proper place? Or . . . or did he mean that sometimes Mr. Longstreet lost his head and then found it again? How was that possible? Wouldn't you need your head to find your head? I was confused.

"Bowser!" Birdie hissed at me. Did I detect a slight whimpering going on, perhaps caused by someone around the table? Couldn't have been me! And if by some crazy chance it was, I put a stop to it right away.

Now Mr. Longstreet turned to the sheriff and there was a flash of an eagle-type glare. "It does not mean that," he said.

"But sometimes?" said the sheriff.

"I don't know where you're going with this."

"Just asking questions. But if they're pointed somewhere, it's to the disappearance—the possible disappearance—of Snoozy LaChance."

"I keep hearing that name," Mr. Longstreet said. "I have yet to meet the man."

"Really?" said the sheriff. "I'm pretty sure Snoozy

would interest you. He's what you might call a fish whisperer, has a flat-out gift when it comes to finding fish in these parts."

"When he's awake," said Perkins.

The sheriff shot Perkins a sharp glance. Perkins looked down.

"Word is that Snoozy got himself hired to one of the bounty hunters," the sheriff continued. "We have evidence that Snoozy and that particular bounty hunter—"

Grammy leaned forward. "What particular bounty hunter are we talking about?"

"That would be Brock Stovall," the sheriff said.

Grammy snorted.

"Uh," said the sheriff, "anything you can tell us about him, ma'am?"

"Screw loose," said Grammy, "which I'd be surprised if you didn't know already."

The sheriff nodded. "Is it a surprise to you that Snoozy would hook up with someone like him?"

"Snoozy's a good man," Grammy told him, "but there's some in these parts that have a knack when it comes to manipulating good men. Especially good men like Snoozy."

"Thanks for that, Miz Gaux," the sheriff said. "Maybe I haven't appreciated how much you must know about our parish."

"We should put her on retainer," Perkins said.

"Pah," said Grammy.

I was totally with Grammy on that one. Nola wore a retainer, no problem, but it wouldn't have been a good look on Grammy.

"Back to Snoozy," said the sheriff. "We have evidence that he and Stovall had a camp set up on Little Flamingo Island. Evidently, there was a period of time when Snoozy was by himself at the camp. That period"—Sheriff Cannon swung around and faced Mr. Longstreet—"coincides with Mr. Longstreet's nearby presence in a pirogue he'd rented out of Baie LaRouche. Mr. Longstreet ended up in possession of a distinctive set of sunglasses that belonged to Snoozy. In this job, we look for motive, means, and opportunity. We've got motive—Mr. Longstreet's hatred of the bounty hunters. We've got opportunity—the two men alone on an island. Means? When we talk about means we're talking how the crime was done, with a weapon, for example. Any help you can give us on that, Mr. Longstreet?"

"I was on the island," said Mr. Longstreet. "I found the sunglasses—exactly how I explained to the child and the large gentleman who was with her—Len, I believe—"

"Lem," said Birdie, but maybe too quiet for anyone but me to hear.

"—on the island," Mr. Longstreet went on. "All the rest of what you've said is absurd speculation. If this Snoozy

236

fellow is indeed in trouble, you're now wasting valuable time."

The sheriff's face got hard, and a vein jumped in the side of Perkins's neck. I got the idea they weren't liking Mr. Longstreet a whole lot. I'd already gotten there myself. "How about we take a short break?" the sheriff said. "Give Mr. Longstreet a few minutes to think things over."

"What is there to think over?" said Mr. Longstreet. "The conclusion's obvious. You have no idea how to conduct an investigation. Here's a suggestion: Go question the bounty hunter."

"Brock Stovall?"

"Exactly."

"In fact, we've done that, but he was never a serious suspect. No motive, Mr. Longstreet. Taking good care of Snoozy was in his best interest, Snoozy being his only shot at winning the bounty. Plus he's been out there searching high and low for Snoozy. Stovall's not clever enough to fake something like that." Sheriff Cannon took a small, shiny machine from his pocket and laid it on the table. "And we're looking for someone clever, no doubt about that. Someone clever enough to throw us off the scent."

Us? Was I included? I'd been thrown off a scent? Wow! That had to be the cleverest human ever to walk the planet! But the truth was I didn't believe it, not for a second.

"We sent the recording of the reassuring call that came

in from Snoozy to the lab in Baton Rouge." The sheriff glanced at Birdie. "On account of questions raised by Birdie, here. She wondered if maybe there was some muffled language we were missing. This is the cleaned-up version the lab sent back."

The sheriff pressed a button and then came Snoozy's voice: "Hello? Hey? Anybody home? This is Snoozy. Snoozy LaChance? From St. Roch? Hi there. The thing is—" Then came a muffled part I remembered, a muffled part with a strange, metallic click, very faint, that I'd missed the first time, followed by Snoozy saying "Don't"—now surely clear to anyone with ears. I took a quick scan around the table. Everyone heard that "Don't," no doubt about it. And it scared Birdie and Grammy: I could see it on their faces. Meanwhile, Snoozy was finishing up. "So don't worry 'bout me. Back just as soon as I get done with this here project. Bye now."

"Thank you, Birdie, for being so thorough," the sheriff said. "'Don't' comes through, loud and clear. Did you catch that click sound right before?"

Birdie nodded.

"What do you think it was?"

"I don't know."

"Pistol getting cocked," Grammy said. She gave Mr. Longstreet a cold look. "Someone had a gun to Snoozy's head."

238

"Claire!" he said. "You can't believe I'd do anything like that."

"The Henry Longstreet I knew way back when could not," Grammy said.

The sheriff gazed at Mr. Longstreet. "What about this Henry Longstreet, right here?"

"You're making one mistake after another," Mr. Longstreet said.

Sheriff Cannon and Officer Perkins rose. The sheriff motioned for Birdie and Grammy. They followed him to the door, and I followed Birdie, somehow getting out first. The sheriff was last. He turned back to Mr. Longstreet.

"Think about your future."

"Am I under arrest?" Mr. Longstreet said.

"Should you be?"

Grammy gave Mr. Longstreet a hard look. "I know my answer to that question."

The sheriff closed the door.

18

FIRST THINGS FIRST: THAT'S ONE OF THE best human ideas going. I thought of it as we all strolled out to the dock in Baie LaRouche, possibly giving Mr. Longstreet a chance to think things over, if I'd understood right. In this case, first things first meant sidling up to Officer Perkins. Here's a tip: When you sidle up to someone, get as close as you can to the pocket where the treats are stashed.

"Hey there, Bowser." Officer Perkins reached down and gave me a pat. "What's doin'?"

Treats. Treats were what's doin'. I nosed up to Officer Perkins's pocket, perhaps shifting his sidearm out of the way. There were biscuits in that pocket, biscuits I liked. They came in that beautiful gold box. We were all out at home, which made this present moment all the more urgent.

"Heh, heh," Perkins said. "I do believe you've sniffed out a biscuit. That correct?"

I wagged my tail. Yes, correct, well done, Officer Perkins. Now can we get on with it?

He gave me a big smile. "How about you do a trick or two, earn your biscuit the honest way?"

Excuse me? Earn my biscuit? Do . . . do a trick? Like roll over, shake, or play dead? I hate doing stupid tricks like that. Wouldn't you? A very bad thought entered my head, something about a trick Officer Perkins and I could perform together, namely knocking him clear off the dock and into the drink. But that wasn't me. Would I ever do a thing like that? No. So . . . it must have been someone else. I wondered who.

Meanwhile, Perkins was laughing his low, rumbly laugh and reaching into his pocket. "Got a real funny look on your mug, pal." He held out the biscuit—yes, the gold-box kind, and not only that but the giant size as well, my favorite biscuit size. I took it in one gentle little motion, nothing greedy about it, and—

"Ow!" said Perkins for some reason.

—and trotted ahead, catching up with Birdie, Grammy, and the sheriff.

"What I'd like to do now is take Birdie over to Little Flamingo Island and have her walk me through the visit she and Lem had there with Longstreet," the sheriff said.

"I'll be coming, too," said Grammy. "But first I'd like a word with Birdie."

241

"Of course," the sheriff said, and he dropped back, joining Officer Perkins.

I thought Perkins said something like, "Got a bandage on you, Sheriff?" But I might have misheard.

A flagpole stood at the end of the dock, a flag fluttering in the breeze. It happened to be that flag you often see in these parts, with the stars and stripes. Not sure what it's about, but I've always liked the look of it. We stood under the fluttering flag.

There wasn't much height difference between Grammy and Birdie anymore, with Birdie growing so fast, and Grammy not growing at all; in fact, maybe shrinking a bit. Other than the height similarity, they didn't look at all like each other, but the way they stood, so straight, was identical.

"Anything you want to say to me, child?" Grammy said.

"Sorry."

"Can't have you jumping onto trucks and going who knows where."

"You're right, Grammy. But I was so worried about Snoozy."

"I am, too. But you're a kid. Maybe you have too much freedom for a kid." For a moment, she gazed over the water, as though looking for something far away. "On the other hand, I had lots of freedom when I was a kid. Were things so different then?"

"I don't know."

"But the both of us know what your mama would think."

Birdie nodded.

"Meaning I should ground you."

"If you say so, Grammy."

"'Course then I'd have to be grounding myself in the bargain."

"Grammy?"

Grammy gave Birdie a close look. Did her old, washed-out blue eyes grow kind of misty? Didn't see that every day. Grammy quickly dabbed her eyes with the back of her arm, a thin, sinewy arm that was still pretty strong.

"I'm sorry, too, Birdie," she said.

"I don't understand. What for?"

"For . . . for what's happened with Henry Longstreet."

"You didn't do anything wrong."

"Oh, but I did. Like a fool—like an old fool—I let him into our lives."

"But he seemed all right, Grammy. And we actually don't know if he's done anything wrong."

"Not true," said Grammy. "What he did on *Bayou Girl* was as wrong as wrong can be."

"Steering it at those boats?"

"Exactly. And not just that. Perkins tells me that there was a struggle at the wheel. Anything to that?"

"A little."

Grammy pointed to Birdie's arm. "That looks like a bruise, a recent type of bruise."

"It's nothing," Birdie said.

"Did he hit you?"

"No, ma'am."

"Or push you? Or get rough in any way?"

Birdie's lower lip started to tremble. I hated seeing that, moved toward her. But Grammy beat me to it! Wow! She took Birdie in her arms before I could even get there.

"That's unforgivable," Grammy said.

Birdie cried a bit. "It's like he's two different people."

"With folks like that, living with a bee in their bonnet, the good part ends up a total waste." Grammy patted Birdie's back. "So it's like this. Either we both get grounded, you and me, or neither one. You pick."

Birdie made a funny noise, part crying, part laughing. "Neither one," she said. I polished off the last crumbs of my biscuit and circled back to see how Officer Perkins was getting along. As for living with a bee in your bonnet, I didn't want to go there, not for a second.

The water-patrol launch—Sheriff Cannon at the wheel, with Officer Perkins staying behind to keep an eye on Mr. Longstreet—made a long, slow curve into the mostly ruined dock on Little Flamingo Island. No flamingos in the two trees at the center of the island this time. I kind of missed them.

Birdie helped the sheriff tie up and then led us along the overgrown path, me actually doing the leading. The scent of Snoozy's Mr. Manly cologne was gone, but there was still a faint smell of gasoline and bait worms. I came oh-so-close to figuring out something very important. Wow! What a lovely feeling, to be at your very sharpest!

We reached the old tumbledown stone hut, roofless and covered in vines. "Here's where Mr. Longstreet brought us," Birdie said. "Lem thought it might go all the way back to the pirates."

"Some people got pirates on the brain," Grammy said.

"In more ways than one," the sheriff said. "The pirate mentality's still alive in these parts."

Grammy turned to him. "Wearing you down, Sheriff?"

"No. Why would you say that?"

"Just wondering how long you plan on sticking with the job."

"That's a strange thought. I've got no plans to leave."

Birdie looked surprised. She opened her mouth as if to say something, then stopped herself.

"Birdie?" said the sheriff. "Something you wanted to say?"

"Um," Birdie said. "Just that"—she gestured through the open doorway of the hut—"Mr. Longstreet told us he found Snoozy's sunglasses in here."

We entered the hut. Nothing much had changed, except there'd been some recent peeing on top of all the peeing that had gone on before. The broken bottles, empty cans, cigarette butts, and busted-up old wooden crate were all as we'd left them.

"He told us the sunglasses were right there," Birdie said. "Beside the crate."

The sheriff squatted down and eyed the crate.

"See the broken ends of those boards?" Birdie said.

"What about them?" said the sheriff.

"Well, the wood is fresh-looking. The rest of the crate's all moldy. I—I think Snoozy was in some kind of fight."

The sheriff nodded.

"But if it was with Mr. Longstreet, then why would he bring us out here to show us the evidence?"

"That kind of thing can happen in this line of work," the sheriff said. "You get a certain type who's . . . how to say it, exactly?"

"Too smart by half," said Grammy.

The sheriff nodded. "That's it. Thank you, ma'am." He turned to Birdie.

"What happened next?"

"Mr. Longstreet showed us the display board out back." We went outside and looked at the plank with the hooks set in it. No sharks hung on them today. "There were sharks on the hooks," Birdie said. "But not bull sharks, and none of them real big."

We gazed at the naked hooks. Everybody got very thoughtful. Well, not me. What was there to think about when it came to empty hooks? I wandered off in no particular direction, soon picked up the faintest possible scent of Mr. Manly, at the very edge of what I can do. I followed the scent down what might have been a path long ago, now mostly scrub. After just a few steps I came upon a red flip-flop. I sniffed it, caught a slightly stronger smell of Mr. Manly. Were red flip-flops important in some way? I tried to remember, my mind going *red flip-flops, red flip-flops* over and over, but nothing coming after that. Except that my mind got tired, and let me know right away that it had had enough thinking for the time being. So, without another thought, I picked up the red flip-flop and trotted back to the tumbledown hut.

". . . right about that, Birdie," the sheriff was saying. "No doubt in my mind now that there was a struggle out here and that Snoozy's in some sort of trouble. Next step is to go back over things with Longstreet."

"Has he done something to Snoozy?" Grammy said, her voice a little wavery, very unusual for her.

"Not saying that," the sheriff said. "And Longstreet may not be the culprit. But I've got a hunch he knows more than he's saying."

"Are you going to arrest him?"

The sheriff shook his head. "Surest way to make him clam up. At least he's talking now."

"But he could leave whenever he wants?" Grammy said.

"Correct."

"Would you arrest him then?"

"Cross that bridge when we come to it," the sheriff said. Was there another way to cross bridges? I got the feeling the sheriff might not be on top of his game today. "I'm counting on his too-smart-by-half side to keep him talking. Meanwhile, you two might as well— Hey there, Bowser." He reached out. "Whatta you got there?"

What I had was not for him. Did Sheriff Cannon really believe I'd be giving him little gifts while Birdie was around? No, not on top of his game today, not close. I sidled over to Birdie, my eyes on the sheriff the whole time in case he was planning a fast one, and laid the red flip-flop at her feet.

"What's this?" she said, picking it up. If she'd sniffed it she would have figured out the answer right away, but the idea didn't seem to occur to her. Or to any of them, for that matter. Not one of them took a single sniff at that flip-flop. Humans could be a puzzle.

"Birdie?" Grammy said. "Remember those flip-flops I gave Snoozy at Christmas last year?"

Birdie squinted inside the flip-flop. *Just smell it!* "Says size seven," Birdie said.

"Snoozy has very small feet for a fellow his height," Grammy said.

"How about we try to locate the other one?" the sheriff said. "Where'd you find this, Bowser?"

I sat down. As if I was suddenly on the sheriff's payroll!

"Bowser!" Birdie said. "You be good!"

I bounced right up and trotted toward the scrubby path. Ol' Bowser: on nobody's payroll, better believe it. At the same time, when Birdie speaks, I listen. I even listen when she's silent. No payroll necessary between me and Birdie.

Soon we were all standing around the spot where I'd found the flip-flop. Birdie, Grammy, and the sheriff split up, went off thrashing around in different directions. I stayed put. No more Mr. Manly smell in the air. This search was going to come up empty, guaranteed.

Some humans give up sooner than others. This little

group we had out in the dense and spiky brush on Little Flamingo Island was the type that gives up later, very much later. But at last, when it was over—no second red flip-flop or anything else at all interesting found, hardly needs mentioning—and they were fanning themselves and passing around a water bottle, the sheriff said, "The flip-flop doesn't really add anything, just confirms what we already know. Namely that Snoozy was here."

"And left in a way I don't like," Grammy said.

"I'm afraid so," said the sheriff.

We pulled away from the dock in Baie LaRouche, Grammy at the wheel and Birdie and me in the bow, Birdie dangling her feet over the side. And me with a couple of paws dangling over the side myself—why leave that out? So much fun to do what Birdie does! Sheriff Cannon and Officer Perkins stayed behind with Mr. Longstreet. The sheriff had asked Grammy if she wanted to say good-bye to Mr. Longstreet and she'd shaken her head. "I'll have something to say to him in due time," she'd said.

And since then she'd been pretty quiet. Birdie and I watched the water, so smooth in the bayou, slipping past the hull of *Bayou Girl*. That sight will put you in a thoughtful mood. No actual thoughts came to me, but I still felt the mood, maybe even better with no thoughts in it. Birdie started singing, her voice quiet, almost a whisper.

"Are you real, Mr. Nice Guy?
Mr. Nice Guy, Mr. Nice Guy,
Or are you a bad, bad dream?"

I chipped in, making musical sounds of my own, a kind of *wee-oo wee-oo*, quite pleasing to my ear. Birdie seemed to like it, too: She gave me a nice little smile. Looking past her, I noticed Grammy watching from her place at the console.

"Birdie?" she said. "Whyn't you come on back here?"

"Sure, Grammy."

We rose, moved along the narrow walkway between the cabin and the outside rail—we've got very good balance on boats, me and Birdie—and joined Grammy.

"Wanna take the wheel?" Grammy said.

"I don't know, Grammy. The legal part, and all."

"Well now, it just so happens that I'm right here. And if you don't drive the boat, how you ever gonna learn?"

"But I already know, kind of."

"All the more reason!" Grammy stepped away from the controls and Birdie took over.

"Same course and speed, Grammy?"

"Yup. Just chuggin' along at a civilized bayou speed, west bank goin' down to the sea, east bank comin' home."

"Red right returning," Birdie said.

"Bingo." Grammy gazed at Birdie's hands on the wheel. *Bayou Girl* likes chuggin' along like this. Feel that in your hands?"

"I think so."

"She's a fine old lady," Grammy said.

"I love her," said Birdie.

We were almost back in St. Roch, the gentle arch of the Lucinda Street Bridge in the distance, when another boat came up quickly from behind. "Darn cowboy," said Grammy.

I checked out this boat as it closed in—an untidy boat of the kind Grammy calls a floating yard sale.

"Hey," Birdie said. "That's *Dixie Flyer.*"

Dixie Flyer pulled toward the middle of the bayou to pass us, its engine making a high whine that I knew was not a good sound. Deke Waylon was at the controls, his stringy hair straight back in the breeze.

"Corner-cutting no-account," Grammy said. We always waved to other boaters. Grammy has two waves—a quick side-to-side for folks she thinks are okay, and a raised and quickly lowered hand for the not okay. Deke Waylon got the second kind. What was this? He didn't wave back, actually turned away and maybe even sped up a little, bluish smoke drifting above the prop wash. *Bayou Girl* rose up in the wake of *Dixie Flyer*, Birdie doing something at the wheel that smoothed everything out.

"Maybe he's mad at us," she said.

"Why?"

"Because Snoozy didn't join up with him for the bounty hunt."

"Then Deke Waylon's an idiot," Grammy said. "Which we already knew. And did you catch the state of that boat of his?"

"Floating yard sale," Birdie said.

"You can say that again." Which Birdie did not. That didn't stop Grammy from going into a long explanation on the meaning of shipshape, complete with many details, all of which I'd heard before, even remembering some of them. But I wasn't really listening. Instead, I was looking ahead at *Dixie Flyer*, now in front of us and moving away fast. There was a big, brass padlock on the cabin door, glinting in the sunshine. It interested me, although I had no idea why.

We passed under the Lucinda Street Bridge. Junior, leaning against the back of the food truck, spotted us, waved wildly, and started running along the path. We were going real slow, almost at the Gaux Family Fish and Bait dock, so he had no trouble keeping up.

"Birdie! Birdie!"

"For goodness' sake," Grammy said, taking over at the wheel, "quiet him down."

Birdie went to the side of the boat. "Hey, Junior."

"Birdie! Birdie!"

"What is it?"

"The contest, Birdie! We're gonna win! I know for sure!"

19

SOME HUMANS ARE KIND OF SLUGGISH, hardly moving at all. Others are just the opposite and don't know how to stop. Junior Tebbets is both! He can lie around on the grass by the food truck not doing a blasted thing, as his dad Wally often says, or he can be like now, inside Gaux Family Fish and Bait, unable to sit still or stand still, bouncing around with a rod in his hand, practicing sideways casts even though there was no reel.

"We're gonna win! We're gonna win!"

Birdie glanced out the sliders at the back, where Grammy was busy hosing down *Bayou Girl*'s deck.

"Songs are coming into my head so fast I don't have time to write them down! And I'm forgetting most of them. But it doesn't matter—more keep coming. What do you think of that?"

"Well . . ."

"We're gonna win, Birdie! And then—watch out, music world!"

"Um, Junior," Birdie said. "What makes you so sure? Have you heard from anybody?"

"Huh? Like who?"

"Like someone at the radio station."

"Not yet. Way too early. But don't you ever just *know* something?"

"Depends what you mean."

"Besides, I had this dream."

"You dreamed we won the contest?"

"Not just that. I mean, that too, yeah. But we were at the Grammys, Birdie! I dreamed we were at the Grammys—me, you, and Nola—and it was so real it had to be true, understand? I had a true dream about the actual future."

I didn't know where to begin. First of all, I, too, had had dreams about being at Grammy's. We live with Grammy, after all, at 19 Gentilly Lane. Second, Junior and Nola had both been at Grammy's in real life, no dreaming necessary. Third, while I'm sure those visits had been pleasant, why all this sudden excitement? I'd always thought I understood Junior pretty well. Now I wasn't so sure.

". . . sparkling golden dress," he was now saying. "You were in these cool ripped jeans and a T-shirt, and I—"

"Nola was wearing a sparkling dress—"

"Golden."

"—and I had on jeans and a T-shirt?"

"The cool ripped kind of jeans."

"You said that."

"I was wearing one of those top hats. We danced around the stage, Birdie! Everyone was cheering like crazy."

Birdie gazed at him. I got the feeling she was about to say something amazing, but at that point she caught a movement over Junior's shoulder. A red convertible was pulling into the lot out front. Did I know this car?

"Junior," Birdie said. "Wait here."

"Huh?"

"I have to deal with this . . . this customer."

Junior turned and looked out. "Cool ride."

"Yeah. I'll be right back."

We headed for the door, me and Birdie.

"What kind of customer?" Junior said, following us.

Birdie raised her hand. "Stay."

I sat right down.

"Not you," Birdie said. "You, Junior. Stay here."

"What's the deep dark secret?"

"There is no . . . Just stay here. Please!"

We went out, the door closing behind us. Right away I caught the strong scent of hair gel, and it all came back to me: The smiling dude now climbing out of the red convertible was Roone K. Knight, program manager at WSBY, Voice of Bayou Country.

"Well hello there, the very appropriately named Birdie," he said. "How you doin' on this lovely day?"

"Uh, good, thanks."

I was doing pretty good myself, although things would have been better if Roone had worn those beautiful two-toned leather shoes instead of the sneakers—no doubt very fancy—that he was sporting today.

"Great to hear," Roone said. "I was in the area and stopped by to see if you had a chance to think about my proposal."

"Yes, sir," Birdie said.

"And?"

"Well, I—I guess what I think is I'd really like to go, especially if Nola and Junior are included."

Roone kept smiling, although his eyes stopped joining in the fun. "Haven't we been through this? I'm afraid that's just not in the cards. This particular opportunity is about you alone."

Then came a silence. Birdie looked down at her feet. "In that case . . ." she said, and stood up very straight. I could feel the effort of that! She looked Roone in the eye, or just about. Maybe more on nose level, to be more accurate. "In that case, the answer is no. No, thank you, sir."

Roone's smile vanished completely. "Sure about that?"

Birdie nodded—a slow sort of nod that didn't look so sure to me.

"Kind of an unusual decision," Roone said. "Can I ask why?"

"We're a band," said Birdie. "Nola, Junior, and me."

"Your call, kid," Roone said. He got into the red convertible and drove off, not checking the rearview mirror even once.

We went back inside the store. Junior was watching through the big front window.

"What was all that about?"

"Nothing," Birdie said.

First thing the next morning Grammy called the sheriff, putting him on speaker so I could hear. Well, maybe so Birdie could hear, too.

"Any news?"

"'Fraid not," the sheriff said. "Didn't get much out of Henry Longstreet and we ended up cutting him loose. But we're keeping an eye on his movements, twenty-four-seven. We've also got a full investigation going on in Baie LaRouche—questioning all the charter and fishing captains, checking closed-circuit video from the docks in the past four days, monitoring radio traffic."

"So you're taking it seriously now," Grammy said.

"I take every investigation seriously, ma'am. And especially this, since Mr. Kronik—" He broke off.

"What about Mr. Kronik?"

"Nothing. We wouldn't want this bounty hunt to lead to any . . . let's call it bad publicity."

"For Mr. Kronik?" Grammy said.

"I was going to say for the parish."

"Were you?"

"Yes, ma'am," the sheriff said. "Got the DA on another line. Good to talk to you."

Click.

Grammy hung up, not gently. She glanced at Birdie. "Something you want to say?"

"Me? Oh, no, not a thing."

"Looked like it there for a moment."

Not long after that, we opened up the shop. Wally Tebbets was the first person through the door. Had he ever bought anything from us? Not that I remembered. That had to mean he was bringing snacks, just out of the goodness of his heart. My mind told me that. My nose told me something different. Wally had no snacks on him, not a crumb. He did have chewing gum stuck to the bottom of one shoe, but I've had a difficult encounter or two with gum and didn't want to go there.

"Morning, everybody," he said. "Lem around?"

Grammy shook her head. "Down in Baie LaRouche, helping out with the search for Snoozy."

"Is he a good driver?"

"Lately, yeah," Grammy said. "Lookin' for a driver?"

"Planning on running a second truck."

"Nice to hear."

"Thanks, ma'am. Any chance Lem's got some cooking skills?"

"Nope."

"Rules him out. I need a driver who can cook."

"I'll ask around."

"Much obliged," Wally said. "I'd also like to rent that jon boat of yours, just for today."

"Nope. We don't rent bareboat here, never have, never will."

"Fine with me. I was thinking maybe Birdie could drive. She old enough?"

"Yes, sir—under ten horse is the rule, and we run a nine point nine on the jon boat."

"Happy to pay her a hundred bucks, plus the boat."

Grammy's eyes narrowed, like maybe she thought Wally was up to something. "Driver compensation is included in the rental."

"Got ya," said Wally.

"Okay then," Grammy said. "Where did you want her to take you?"

"Not me, exactly. This food truck I'm talkin' about's gonna be for up in Betencourt Bridge, what with the construction, the call centers and all. Thought I might send

Junior up there with some samples, sell 'em to the workers at cost, prime the pump. Junior on his own, of course, is one thing. Junior with Birdie along—well, that's another."

They both turned to Birdie.

"Well, Birdie?" Grammy said. "Up to you."

"You could start a whole food-boat business, Mr. Tebbets—to go with the truck!"

"Right there is what I'm talking about," said Mr. Tebbets.

"Wanna make up another song on the ride?" Junior said.

"No," said Birdie.

We were aboard the jon boat, Junior on the bench seat in the bow, Birdie steering in the stern, me beside her. In the center of the boat stood three big coolers, one packed with shrimp po'boys, one with Wally's Secret Recipe po'boys, and one with drinks on ice. Birdie had the cash box between her feet.

"Something about boat rides makes you want to make up songs," Junior said. "Just gliding along, nice and peaceful." He reached over the side, trailed his hand in the water. "How come they call it a jon boat?"

"No idea."

Junior glanced around. "It's not bumpy, like other boats."

"We're on the bayou, Junior. And there's no wind."

Birdie checked the sky. Hey! Hadn't the sun been shining when we got up? Now it was wall-to-wall clouds, not the puffy white kind, but gray and flat. "Any kind of waves and it gets real bumpy on a jon boat."

"Yeah?"

"On account of the flat bottom. It's for calm waters."

"Calm waters," Junior said. "That's our title, right there."

"Title for what?"

"The song we're making up."

"Junior? Do you even listen to people?"

"About what?"

Birdie raised her voice. With anyone else, you might have said she sounded crabby, but Birdie can't sound crabby. "I don't want to make up a song. Do you read me?"

"Not really. We're musicians, after all."

"Not me," Birdie said. "I'm not a musician."

"Okeydokey artichokey."

"And if you say that again, you're going over the side."

"Say what?" Junior grinned a big grin, like he'd come out on top. I waited for Birdie to say whatever it was she didn't want him to say, but she shot him an angry look— an angry look from Birdie!—and . . . and then suddenly froze, her gaze on Junior's feet. He wore flip-flops, one black and one red.

"Junior? What's with the flip-flops?"

"Huh?"

"They don't match. One's black and one's red."

Junior checked out his flip-flops. "True."

"How come?"

"How come what?"

"Let me see the red one."

"Huh?"

Birdie throttled back, walked up to the bow, and took the red flip-flop right off Junior's foot. She gave it a close look. "Size seven."

"That's my size."

"Where'd you get it?"

"Search me."

"Think, Junior. There must be some story."

"Why?"

"Because they don't match! Whoa—did Nola say something about that?"

"Search me."

"Think, Junior!"

Junior shut his eyes tight, not a pleasant visual, at least not on him. "No clue. Why is it important? Wait—you're saying there's a song in it?"

A little muscle bunched in Birdie's jaw. I'd never seen that before. She dropped the red flip-flop on the deck, went back to the stern, and got us under way again. The trip seemed to take a long time. That can happen when humans aren't on speaking terms, especially if, like me on that jon boat trip, you don't know why. But finally the bayou opened up into a sort of lake with a small town on one side and lots of big yellow earthmovers busy at the far end.

"Can I ask where we are?" Junior said. "Without getting my head bit off?"

Whoa! I looked around for any creature big enough to do that, and saw none. There are a lot of false alarms in human life.

"Betencourt Bridge," Birdie said, heading toward a long dock extending out from the shore.

"Where's the bridge?"

"Blown up in the Civil War."

"Why?"

"Why? What kind of question is that? Things get blown up in wars, bridges especially."

Junior gazed out at the lake. "So it's down there, on the bottom?"

"Huh?"

"The bridge."

"I guess so. The remains, the metal parts anyway. Wood rots fast around here. Grab that line and hop up on the dock when I pull alongside."

Junior's eyes were still on the water. "The bridge across the bottom of the lake," he said softly, and then began humming a little tune.

"Junior! On the dock! Now!"

Junior sort of snapped awake, even though he hadn't been sleeping, and jumped onto the dock.

"The line!"

"Line?"

"You forgot the bowline!"

"Oops."

And then came several other missteps—and Birdie, just like Grammy, hates missteps on boats, above all on landings, which had better be smooth and bumpless, or else—but finally we were squared away. Birdie set up the umbrella that Wally had put in the boat, an umbrella bearing a picture of his food truck, and Junior unloaded the coolers. I sat and watched a frog who was also sitting, but on a lily pad in the water. Something about him just sitting there like he owned the place bothered me. I began making plans.

Here's something you may not know about frogs: They can be hard to sneak up on. That was why I needed to do my most careful thinking, but I didn't have a chance, because customers started showing up almost right away. They were all workers in hard hats and grimy boots, and more than one of them—in fact, just about every single one—looked at the umbrella and said, "Food truck? More like a food boat!" Or something close to that. And Junior laughed every time, even slapped his knees once or twice, like it was the funniest joke he'd ever heard. I didn't get it. Neither did Birdie, who didn't laugh even once.

Maybe she was simply too busy with that cash box. Were we selling or what? Po'boys were just flying out of those coolers—actually flying when Junior started tossing them to customers, some of those tosses not very good. Birdie put a stop to that. She stood by a bollard, the cash box on top, and counted out change the way Grammy had taught her. "One shrimp po'boy at four ninety-five. Out of twenty. There's a nickel, plus five and ten makes twenty. Thank you, ma'am." Plus there were tips, which Birdie kept in a paper cup on another bollard. In short, we were raking it in! Humans love raking it in. You can see it on their faces. Is it the best human look? Maybe not.

Finally, there was a little pause and Junior took a swing at counting the money, but he lost track and ended up saying "Wow!" and closing the box. Birdie took it and replaced it on the bollard, keeping her hand on top.

"You're in a bad mood, huh?" Junior said.

"No."

"You're not laughing at the food-boat joke."

"You think it's funny?"

"Sure," said Junior, "especially when they all say it."

"Hrrmf."

What was this? Birdie saying "hrrmf"? The only hrrmfing human I'd ever heard was Grammy. I tried to take the next step but couldn't think what it was.

More customers showed up. The very first one ordered a Secret Recipe po'boy, glanced at the umbrella, and said, "Food truck? More like a food boat!"

Junior laughed and slapped his knee. Birdie just stood there, stony-faced. But then, all of a sudden, like something bright got switched on inside, her whole expression changed and she started laughing. First, just a small laugh, but it grew and grew and soon she was laughing harder than I'd ever seen her laugh, tears streaming down her cheeks. The folks in the line laughed, too, even the newcomers who hadn't heard the joke and couldn't have known what was going on. I myself ran around crazily and then sprang into the water and went after that frog. He gazed at me in an unfriendly way until I was real close, then dove off the lily pad. A lazy kind of dive, in truth, more like a plop. The frog plopped off the lily pad in the most infuriating way and vanished in the lake.

Not long after that, we sold out—good timing, Birdie said, because the weather was changing.

"It is?" Junior said.

He glanced up at the sky, much darker now, and lower, if that makes any sense. Plus the wind was rising, the surface of the lake getting choppy. Junior packed up the umbrella. Birdie emptied the paper cup in her lap and was dividing the tip money when a boat motoring toward the opposite shore caught her eye.

"Recognize that boat?" she said.

Junior peered across the lake. "Nope."

"You were on it," Birdie said. "It's *Dixie Flyer*."

"Just another brave incident in my life." Junior loaded the coolers on the jon boat, stashed the umbrella under the seats. Rain began to fall, not hard, but cold, and slanting sideways. Junior took another look at *Dixie Flyer* and went still.

"Hey! Guess what."

"Just spit it out."

Spitting was going to happen now? I wasn't a big fan, although it's always interesting to watch spit hitting the water. I'd seen a lot of that, living on the bayou. But Junior didn't take up Birdie's invitation. Instead, he pointed to *Dixie Flyer*.

"Funny thing about that brave incident, now that I think. Like, at the same time as I was thinking about the red flip-flop, if you see what I mean."

"I don't," Birdie said.

"Like . . . like two trains meeting up. But not crashing. Since it's going on inside my head."

"You lost me, Junior."

"Pretty simple. Remember when I jumped on *Dixie Flyer*?"

"The brave incident."

"Yeah. Well, when I was on board, in that cabin, I noticed that one of my flip-flops had fallen off. So I reached around with my foot and slipped it back on."

Birdie's eyes opened wide.

"A few days later," Junior continued, "I happened to notice that my flip-flops didn't exactly match. One black, one red. Not a big deal, right? Who cares? But now that the trains are meeting . . ."

"You're telling me you picked up that red flip-flop in the cabin on *Dixie Flyer*?"

"Looks that way," said Junior. "Is it important?"

20

THE WIND PICKED UP, DRIVING THE RAIN IN our faces as we motored into the lake, Junior in the bow, Birdie steering in the stern, and me sitting up straight beside her. At the same time, the sky darkened even more, trailing curtains of black cloud almost right down to the water.

"Can't see a thing," Junior said, shielding his eyes. The rain was doing funny things to his Mohawk.

"Good," Birdie said. "That means we can't be seen."

"Hadn't thought of that," Junior said. I was with him on that. In the distance, *Dixie Flyer* appeared in a dim sort of way from between a pair of those cloudy curtains and then vanished behind another one. Rain and wind blotted out all other sound. I couldn't hear *Dixie Flyer*'s engine, could barely hear our own. Meanwhile, we were bumping around pretty good.

"Birdie?" Junior said, both hands holding tight to the edge of the bow seat.

"Yeah?"

"Are we gonna tip?"

"No."

We motored on, the weather getting worse, visibility now down to a small circle with our boat in the middle.

"Birdie?"

"Yeah?"

"I'm feeling kind of pukey."

"Stick your head over the side."

"You mean just go ahead and puke?"

"But not in the boat."

"Will I feel better?"

"For a few minutes."

"Then I'll be pukey again?"

And there was more back and forth about puking, which I tried to tune out because it was making me a bit pukey myself. The jon boat plunged ahead, bouncing up and down, the cooler sliding this way and that.

"Can you make those coolers fast, Junior?" Birdie said.

"How?"

"Bungee cords are in that locker under your seat."

"I've never used bungee cords," Junior said, making no move to open the locker. His eyes and mouth were open wide. Was he scared? I thought so. Did that mean he didn't trust Birdie? I trusted her with all my heart, so I wasn't the least bit scared. She leaned slightly forward, one hand on the steering lever, the other on her knee, and peered into the murk and the rain, her eyes—the blue of the summer sky—the only color around. Except for the red flip-flop on one of Junior's feet. Had I found another one just like it somewhere? I thought and thought and . . . and it came to me! Yes! On Little Flamingo Island! I'd done good.

"Look at Bowser," Birdie said.

"What about him?" said Junior.

"His tail."

"It's wagging?"

"He loves rough weather. Bowser's a born sailor."

Wait a minute. Was that how come my tail had been wagging? I wasn't sure, but if Birdie said so, then that was that. Rough weather was the best! I put my front paws up on the gunwale and wagged my head off. Does that even make sense, since it was the tail I was wagging? It did to me at the time.

Up ahead, the rainy curtains parted again, and we caught a glimpse of the far shore, a swampy dark green forest with no sign of houses or buildings of any kind. *Dixie Flyer* was tied up at a stone landing, and a wiry dude with stringy hair, now plastered to his head, was making his way up a narrow path through the trees. He disappeared around a bend. The rainy curtains closed.

"Are you shivering?" Junior said.

"No," said Birdie.

"You've got goose bumps."

Birdie shrugged. You had to admire her coolness in the face of a terrible insult. If Junior had accused me of being like a goose in any way, he'd have regretted it, and pronto. No end to the unpleasant things I could tell you about geese, but that will have to wait, because all at once the stern of *Dixie Flyer* rose up out of the fog right in front of us. Birdie swung our bow hard to one side and throttled way back. We put-putted slowly past *Dixie Flyer* and approached the stone landing. Here, so close to shore, the wind died down a bit, smoothing out the water. The hull of the jon boat just kissed the landing, Grammy-style, and we came to rest.

"Hitch us to that cleat, Junior," Birdie said, her voice low.

"I'm still a bit pukey."

"And don't forget to take the line."

Junior climbed onto the landing, got everything right the first time. We walked along the landing, all of us soaked from the rain, and approached *Dixie Flyer*. Birdie knocked against the hull with her fist. "Snoozy?" she said, in that strange, whispering shout. "Snoozy?"

No sound on *Dixie Flyer*. I caught a whiff of Mr. Manly in the air, quite faint, pretty much smothered by the smell of gasoline and bait worms.

We gazed into the boat—me with my front paws on the

gunwale, the only way I could see over the side. No one on the boat that I could see. The door to the cabin was closed. Had it been padlocked at some point? I kind of thought so.

"Snoozy?" Birdie called, louder this time. "Snoozy?"

No response.

"How about hopping on board and taking a quick peek into the cabin?" Birdie said.

"After what happened the last time?" said Junior. "No way."

"That's fair," Birdie said. She climbed on board, meaning I did, too, as you must have guessed.

"But the good news is I'm not pukey anymore," Junior called after us.

Birdie turned the knob on the cabin door. It wasn't locked. We looked inside. No one there, and the Mr. Manly smell was faint. We hopped down onto the landing and headed for the narrow path through the trees, in my case because Birdie was doing it and Birdie for reasons unknown to me.

"We're going up the path?" Junior said.

"You don't have to," Birdie said over her shoulder.

Junior ended up coming with us. The trees blocked some of the wind and rain, but if you looked up you saw the tree-tops whipping around crazily. I tried not to look. We rounded the bend where the stringy-haired dude—had to be Deke Waylon, unless I was completely out of the picture—had disappeared, and then another bend, and came to a clearing with a dirt road on the other side. In the middle of the clearing stood a small trailer, the silver teardrop kind, although this one was more rusted than silvery. There was a side door, padlocked with a shiny brass padlock, and a big, round window, with a closed curtain on the inside. Rain pounded on the roof of the trailer. We stood in the trees at the edge of the clearing. I could feel Birdie thinking.

After a few moments, Junior stepped into the clearing. Birdie grabbed his arm and pulled him back. Junior opened his mouth to say something, but right then, from close by, came the sound of a motorcycle revving up. Out from behind the other side of the trailer, the motorcycle appeared, big and black with fat tailpipes, Deke Waylon up top. He turned onto the dirt road and drove off. The throb of the bike's engine got softer and softer, finally losing itself in the sound of the rain, even to my ears.

We left the shelter of the trees and crossed the clearing. Birdie knocked on the door. "Snoozy? Snoozy?"

Silence from inside the trailer.

Birdie raised her voice. "Snoozy!"

More silence. And then came a sort of sound—a human sound but not what you'd call speech, close to a *grrr* but not a *grrr*, somewhat like moans, but not moans, either.

"Snoozy? Is that you?"

Now there were strange thumps.

"Snoozy? Is it you? Can you talk?"

The thumps got louder. Birdie tugged at the padlock. Nothing doing. She glanced at the dirt road. No action there.

"Junior?" She turned to him. "What if we—"

Junior already had a big rock in his hand.

"Yeah, that," Birdie said.

We backed up a little. Junior hurled the rock at the window, missing completely the first time, in fact, missing the whole trailer. But he was on target the second time. The window got smashed to smithereens in a very satisfying way. Birdie cleared off a few stray shards of glass and pushed the curtain aside. We looked in.

A bunk bed stood in the trailer. Snoozy lay on the bottom bunk, handcuffed to a wooden support post for the bunk above. A strip of duct tape sealed off his mouth. He saw us and his eyes seemed to be saying all sorts of things, exactly what, I didn't know, but every bit of it urgent. We climbed in through the broken window, me actually leaping, if you want the real story.

Birdie hurried over to Snoozy and pulled off the duct tape.

"Ouch," Snoozy said. And then, "Ah, that's better. Thanks, Birdie."

She put a hand on his shoulder. He sat up, but not all the way, on account of being handcuffed.

"So happy to see you, Birdie. How did you find me?"

"A long story," Birdie said. "We've got to get you out of here. Where's the key?"

Snoozy glanced at the handcuffs. "Deke's got them." He twisted around toward the door. "Where is he?" Snoozy sounded scared. I'd never heard that from him before. Also he looked scared. A scared-looking Snoozy didn't even seem like Snoozy. I felt bad.

"Gone somewhere on his bike," Birdie said.

The sound of the rain on the trailer's metal roof was like . . . like being inside a drum. It made me edgy, interfered with my thinking ability. My only idea was to try chewing through the handcuffs. Not my best idea ever—I knew that at the time. That was when Junior stepped forward to save the day.

"Let's take the bed frame apart and slide the cuffs right off!"

"Great idea!" said Birdie.

"He keeps a toolbox under the bed," Snoozy said.

Junior got down on his hands and knees and rummaged under the bed.

"What's going on, Snoozy?" Birdie said. "Did he kidnap you? On Little Flamingo Island?"

278

"How do you know?" Snoozy said.

Birdie made a little throwaway gesture with her hand. "But why, Snoozy? Why did he do it?"

"For the bounty, of course. He's kind of angry."

"Because Brock Stovall hired you first?"

"That's right. How come you know so much about it?"

"I don't," Birdie said. "Why has he got you like this? Are you a prisoner?"

"I guess you could say that," said Snoozy. "It's on account of I refused."

"You refused to help him on the bounty hunt?"

"I promised Brock first. Gave my word, if you see what I'm saying. Maybe sort of a jerk—Brock, I mean—but I know him. Don't know Deke—at least I didn't—and he's a jerk, too, even jerkier."

Junior emerged from under the bed with a saw in his hand. "Never used one of these," he said, "but I've seen it done." He made sawing motions in the air. "My dad built the whole back of the food truck from scratch. Not much to it, really." Junior approached the support post that Snoozy was handcuffed to and took what you might call a sawing swing at it. Then came a sort of clang and the saw flew across the room.

"Junior! We don't have time for this." Birdie went and grabbed the saw, started sawing away at the post with long, clean strokes, faster and faster, sawdust jetting out of the cut she was making. With the noise of the saw, plus the rain on the roof, I maybe didn't hear what I should have been hearing.

"Funny thing is," Snoozy said, "I know this bull shark with the lopsided grin."

"You do?" Birdie said.

The post split apart. Birdie pushed the top part aside. The top bunk sagged down. At the same time, Snoozy sat up straight and slid his cuffed hands over the bottom section of the post.

"Been tracking him for years—that lopsided grin makes it easy," Snoozy said, starting to rise. "I even know his favorite hangout, by this ledge where—"

Right then, or maybe just before, was when the door opened. There stood Deke, soaking wet, a gun in his hand, pointed down for the time being.

"Go on, Snooze," he said. "Don't let me interrupt."

21

SOMETIMES TWO THINGS HAPPEN AT ONCE. This was one of those times, and here are the two things: One, Birdie gripped my collar and held tight. Two, I got the very strong urge to spring across the trailer and bite down pretty much my hardest on Deke Waylon's gun hand. But now how was I going to do that?

"Go on, Snoozy," Deke said, "let your buddy Deke in on the secret. Where's this bull shark you suddenly seem to know all about."

Snoozy said nothing. I thought I could feel his mind at work.

"See, now my feelings are hurt," Deke said. "Sharing secrets with these kids here, but freezing me out. Not good for your health, not good at—" He stopped talking, took a close look at Birdie. "Do I know you?"

Like Snoozy, Birdie remained silent. I could feel her mind working, too, at a somewhat faster pace than Snoozy's.

The expression in Deke's eyes changed and became . . . fox-like? Yes, fox-like! And all at once I understood Deke real well, on account of my many experiences with foxes. We've even got foxes in these parts that can climb trees. Just imagine how irritating that can be! But if you know foxes at all then I don't need to tell you how tricky they are. Deke Waylon's eyes showed me he was just like that, only more so.

"Thought I recognized you," he said. "The Gaux kid. What's your first name?"

"You have no right to keep us here," Birdie said.

"Rights?" said Deke. "All anyone's ever done is try and take 'em away from me." He smiled. A wiry dude, not big, but all muscle and bone. Very slowly he held up the gun, kind of loose in his hand and not pointed at anybody. "See this here? That's all you need to know about my rights. Now, I asked you your name and I ain't gonna ask again."

Birdie was silent. The gun seemed to hold her gaze. Me and my kind can smell human fear, and I smelled it now from Birdie. Nothing I could do about it at the moment, not with Birdie holding on to my collar, but way down deep in me—a place where the very important things that just can't be forgotten get stored—I began making plans for Deke.

Meanwhile, Birdie's gaze at last moved away from the gun. She stood real straight and said, "Birdie Gaux," in a way that let me know one more time that she was just the best.

"That's better," Deke said, and turned to Junior. "And you?"

"Junior Tebbets," Junior said, without even the slightest hesitation. He met Deke's foxy, mean eyes for the briefest possible time and quickly added, "Well, actually Wallace Garnet Tebbets Junior, but everyone calls me Junior."

"You seem like a sensible type, Junior." Deke looked at Birdie and Snoozy. "You two gonna be the same?"

"I don't know what you mean," Birdie said.

"But Snoozy does. Tell her, Snooze."

Snoozy shook his head.

"Aw, how touching," said Deke. "Okay, Birdie Gaux, here's how it is. Snoozy here flat-out refused to help me on the bounty hunt. Despite some gentle encouragement, just slapping him around a bit, didn't even leave a mark. Ain't that true, Snooze?"

Snoozy looked down at the floor and didn't answer.

"But here's my guess. Snoozy's one of those gentlemen who wouldn't want to see any of that gentle encouragement applied anywheres else. Catch my drift?"

Right then I saw something brand-new: a hot flash of anger in Snoozy's eyes. He nodded yes.

"Well, well," Deke said. "We're gettin' somewheres at last. Gonna find that bull shark for me, Snoozy? It's in this here lake, ain't it?"

"Yes," said Snoozy. "I'll tell you exactly where if you let us go."

Deke shook his head. "You're gonna show me."

Snoozy thought about that. "All right, but there's no reason you can't cut the kids loose."

Deke smiled his little smile again. "Wouldn't be the right play."

Not long after that we were all aboard *Dixie Flyer* and under way, headed toward the far end of the lake, where the big yellow earthmovers worked. Even though it was still daytime, they weren't working now. At least, not that I could hear. As for seeing them, or seeing pretty much anything: impossible. What we had going down now was a full-blown storm, the wind making high-pitched sounds that hurt my ears, the rain driving sideways, cold and hard, and the waves raised up to human height. We'd never gone out in bad weather, me and Birdie—a no-no at Gaux Family Fish and Bait—but we'd been caught by surprise squalls a few times, and one thing I knew right away: *Dixie Flyer*, around the same size as *Bayou Girl*, did not handle rough going as well, not even close.

Deke was at the controls, so he had a bit of protection from the T-top; but up front in the bow—Deke didn't want anyone behind him in the stern—the rest of us were totally exposed. Maybe I should mention that there was only one life jacket on board, and Deke was wearing it. We all held on tight to something, except for me—holding on is a bit of a challenge, unless I bring my teeth into play. But Birdie had my collar, so I was good. The bow rose way up on a wave, then crashed down, water slopping right over us.

"What's with this boat, Snoozy?" Birdie said. "It's so sluggish."

"Bilge fillin' up," he said.

"Oh my god!" said Junior. "With what?"

"Water," Snoozy told him. "Rainwater. Deck leaks. Rain flows right on through, and the bilge pump's busted."

Birdie glanced back at Deke, the wind tearing at his long, stringy hair, and all the bones of his face somehow showing under the surface, not a pleasant sight. "Does he know?" she said.

"Don't know much when it comes to boat maintenance," Snoozy said.

Birdie's gaze stayed on Deke. "Even if he gets the shark, why would he let us go?"

"After all this, you mean?" Snoozy touched Birdie's shoulder. "Let's not think about that."

Dixie Flyer wobbled up another wave, even bigger than the one before, and crashed down even harder on the other side, this time another wave coming right away and slamming over the bow. It knocked us all back against the front of the cabin, tangled together in a soaking-wet ball. Snoozy grabbed a rail and pulled himself up.

"Deke! Turn back! Your boat can't handle this!"

"Don't tell me about my boat!" Deke shouted. He raised the gun. "Just do your job. Where's my shark?"

Snoozy turned toward the bow and pointed ahead, where there was nothing to see but flying water from above and below. *Dixie Flyer*'s engines were making a strange *throb throb blank throb throb blank* sound, and we kept sort of sliding sideways.

"Keep us straight!" Snoozy shouted.

"Shut your mouth!" Deke shouted right back. He fought with the wheel, got us straightened out, at least partly. But behind him things didn't look so good to me: The top of the transom was real low in the water. "How much farther?" Deke yelled.

"Not much," Snoozy said.

"Then get the rig ready! What's wrong with you?"

Snoozy, almost on his hands and knees, scrambled over to a side locker. As he reached out to raise the top, the wind tore his T-shirt right off him, revealing all his fish tattoos, including the half-finished Mr. Nice Guy on his chest. A half-finished Mr. Nice Guy, maybe, but through the rain he looked like he was on the move.

"Are we gonna sink, Birdie?" Junior said. Me and Birdie were now pressed against him, jammed against another locker farther forward.

"We'll be okay as long as the engines are running." Birdie took Junior's hand. He held on tight.

Snoozy grabbed a long, heavy line and a bucket from the locker. The line had a big, wicked-looking hook at the end. Snoozy opened the bucket, took out a huge bloody hunk of fish meat, and drove the hook deep into it. And just in time, because the boat rose suddenly—and, for the first time, fully sideways to the waves—and tipped way over, the bucket sliding over the side, splashing fish blood everywhere, and throwing me, Birdie, and Junior against the cabin wall.

Dixie Flyer righted herself, real slow. The engines went *throb blank throb blank throb*. Snoozy came forward, coiling the line.

"Snoozy?" Birdie said. "Is the shark really here? Grammy says it can't get into the lake."

"True in the old days, Birdie." Snoozy fastened the end of the line to a cleat, tying on nice and tight. "But water's been rising the past few years."

"How's that possible?"

"Don't know. Maybe the land is sinkin'. All's I know is I see it happening." Snoozy turned to Deke. "Right about here."

Deke backed off on the throttles.

"Snoozy!" Birdie said. "He's throttling down."

"I know."

"But nothing will run out of the bilge. It'll fill up even quicker."

Snoozy glanced at Deke. Deke's face had gone all wild. He was way beyond talking to. "We'll just have to catch this shark quicker than that," Snoozy said.

"All set?" Deke called.

"All set," said Snoozy.

"NOW!"

Snoozy hurled the baited hook over the side. It disappeared in the storm, the storm so loud now I didn't even hear the splash. The coil of line ran out real fast, making a small screaming sound pretty much lost in the storm's roar.

"You done it?" Deke called.

Snoozy nodded.

Deke backed off the throttles even more. I got the feeling we'd stopped going anywhere except for up and down and side to side.

Snoozy glanced back at the transom. Waves were starting to lip over the top.

"More throttle," he said.

"Don't tell me how to do my job!"

"But the bilge is fillin' up. You're gonna sink us, man."

Deke grabbed a long wooden-handled gaff, came forward, the gun now tucked inside his belt, but that mean-looking gaff held high.

"I'll do the thinkin' here, understood?"

Snoozy nodded.

Deke turned to the line, hanging over the side. The engines went *blank blank throb, blank blank throb. Dixie Flyer* rocked from end to end, rolled from side to side, all those movements slow and heavy. Birdie had one hand on the side rail and one on my collar. Everyone else held on to something, except for Deke, standing with his feet wide apart, crouched low—like . . . some creature made for storms like this.

Deke raised his voice over it. "Sure this is the spot?"

"Yup," Snoozy said. "But you're gonna have to throttle up and circle around. Otherwise—"

Deke smacked Snoozy across the face with the back of his hand. That enraged me! I barked my most savage bark. Birdie's hand tightened to the max around my collar. A wave crashed over the transom. And at that moment, Snoozy's line suddenly went taut.

Deke's eyes opened wide. I saw an expression on his face I'd never seen before, a scary combination of joy, greed, and craziness. "YAH! I got 'im!"

We all turned toward the rail and peered over the side. Waves so big, so much rain: It was almost like we were underwater, way down deep. But no. There was still a sort of surface, which I only realized when something huge with an enormous lopsided grin and terrible little eyes came bursting through. It was Mr. Nice Guy, the bloody piece of fish meat between his teeth. Rows and rows of teeth, each and every one big and sharp.

"I GOT 'IM!"

Deke dropped the gaff, began pulling on the line with all his strength.

"No!" Snoozy reached out. "Wait! He's not really hooked—it's just caught in that scar. You'll—"

Deke batted Snoozy's hand away, hauled on the line with all his strength. Mr. Nice Guy didn't like that, as anyone could have seen from how his eyes got even more furious than they already were. But Deke did not see, and he kept hauling on that line, his feet braced halfway up the side.

"Stop!" Snoozy screamed, and the storm screamed even louder. "You'll—"

All at once, Mr. Nice Guy twisted around and dove straight down. The line made a screeching sound and the other side of the boat tipped straight up and now loomed right over our heads. The engines died completely—*blank blank blank.*

290

"We're goin' over!" Snoozy yelled.

"Junior!" Birdie said. "Take a deep breath!"

"I GOT 'IM!"

And then we were upside down. Well, to be more accurate, *Dixie Flyer* was upside down, and I seemed to be under the top of her deck, if that makes any sense. Very hard to see down there, but I knew I was under the boat because every time I tried to swim up I kept bumping my head.

Air! Air! I needed air so bad. I did my dog paddle like never before, kind of frantic, and bumped my head again, and again, and again! And then something amazing happened. I heard Birdie's voice, even though it was impossible to hear anything except the pounding of the storm. *Bowser. It's okay. Stay calm.*

Just like that I was calm. I stopped swimming so frantically and paddled in my normal way. And in what seemed like no time at all, I popped to the surface and breathed in lovely air. No chance to enjoy it, because a wave grabbed me and raised me up high. From there I spotted Birdie, not far away, and Junior beside her. Just then Snoozy bobbed up, too, on the same wave as me, but lower down. Things surfaced around us—plastic bottles, seat cushions, the wooden-handled gaff. There was no sign at all of *Dixie Flyer* or of Deke.

Snoozy and I swam over to Birdie and Junior. I put my

paw on her shoulder and licked her face. *Birdie! Birdie! Birdie!* Nothing else was going on in my mind at that moment.

"Easy, Bowser, easy. We've got to stay—"

I never learned what that was going to be about, because a wave came bashing over us, and another wave rose high above, and in the middle of that wave, his head sticking right out into the air, was Mr. Nice Guy, now free of the hook. He made a snapping motion with his huge mouth, and . . . and what looked like a tangle of long, stringy hair attached to some bloody skin disappeared down Mr. Nice Guy's throat.

Junior screamed. Snoozy's eyes opened wide in terror. I barked a bark that meant business in no uncertain terms, and bared my teeth, just to show Mr. Nice Guy he wasn't the only one bringing a mouthful of sharpies to the table. The wooden-handled gaff floated by. Birdie grabbed it.

Our wave rose up. Mr. Nice Guy's wave came down. Those little eyes were on us, no doubt about that, and they liked what they saw. Mr. Nice Guy shot toward us, his mouth, bleeding from the lopsided scar, wide open. There was lots of screaming—by Junior, maybe by Snoozy, and I barked a bark that sounded kind of scream-like—and at the last second Mr. Nice Guy twisted around and went straight for Birdie. The look on her face! I'll never forget it. Was she afraid? Oh, yeah, but there was something else, something so hard and determined, the face of someone fighting back.

Fighting back: What a beautiful thing to see! Birdie held that gaff in both hands, so steady in all the wild commotion. At the very last moment, when Mr. Nice Guy was almost on top of her, she struck with all her might, jabbing him right on the nose with the metal end of the gaff. The rounded part of the hook, not the sharp part. How was that going to do any good? But then came a surprise. Mr. Nice Guy hit the brakes. His little eyes looked kind of confused. Birdie bopped him again, even harder this time. Mr. Nice Guy got the message. He turned, dove, and vanished into the depths.

We waited in silence, treading water, peering all around, but mostly down, down into the deep. Whatever was happening in the depths seemed to be staying down there.

"Wow!" said Snoozy, shouting over the storm. "How'd you know to do that?"

"Grammy," Birdie told him. "Bull sharks are used to prey that turns tail. Anything else makes them cautious."

"That Grammy!" Snoozy said. "Thinks like a fish!"

He gathered up some seat cushions. I got my front paws on one of them. We rode those seat cushions through the rest of the storm, with only Junior glancing back from time to time. The storm died down pretty quick, like it knew the excitement was over. Soon the shoreline came in view, surprisingly close. We swam onto a small, sandy beach.

Birdie, Junior, and Snoozy sat on the beach, all of them looking kind of dazed. I myself did what I always do after coming out of the water. I gave myself a real good shake, probably the best one of my whole life, spraying drops in all directions and then some. A ray of sunshine poked through the clouds and printed a rainbow over those airborne water drops. My water drops, by the way. Wow! What's more fun than making rainbows?

Divers spotted the wreckage of *Dixie Flyer* down at the bottom of the lake, but the body of Deke Waylon was never seen again. Neither was there ever another sighting of Mr. Nice Guy, but Mr. Kronik said that without some proof he was dead there'd be no bounty payout. That didn't seem to bother Snoozy. He decided to leave the Mr. Nice Guy tattoo on his chest the way it was, half-finished. Pretty soon, folks began arriving at the store to see it. Many, many folks. Lem decided to charge them five bucks a pop, ten if they wanted Snoozy's autograph as well. We had lines out the door, day after day. Snoozy wanted to split the take with Birdie. Grammy put a stop to that in no uncertain terms.

Grammy and Mr. Longstreet went out for coffee and had a long talk. I don't know what it was about, but he left for California the next day. Grammy was quiet for some time after that and then returned to her normal self. Some of us, mostly me, quickly got in trouble for this and that.

Nola and Birdie and me went for a nice walk. Not along the bayou—me and Birdie weren't quite in the mood for the bayou, for some reason—but on a trail on the dry side of town.

"Anything you'd like to tell me, Birdie?" Nola said.

"About what?"

"Oh, anything."

"Not that I can think of."

"Did I ever mention Dahlia?" Nola said.

"Nope."

"Dahlia's my mom's old college roommate. She works at WSBY."

"Oh?"

"Yeah. Oh. So I happen to know about Roone K. Knight."

"Oh?"

"Yeah. Oh. Here's the thing: We're friends for life. So don't screw this up. Take the offer."

Birdie's eyes filled with tears. "But . . . but what about Junior?"

"Junior?" said Nola. "He thinks he's a genius. Nothing you do or don't do will ever change that."

Birdie laughed, a sort of laughing and crying at the same time. She threw her arms around Nola and gave her a big hug. Nola gave her a big hug back. What was this about? I had no idea. All I knew—after a generous amount of time—was that this hugging had gone on plenty long enough, meaning long enough without me. I squeezed in between them.

acknowledgments

Many thanks to my wonderfully astute editor Rachel Griffiths, and to Maya Marlette and the whole team at Scholastic; plus a shout-out to Mylo, a four-footed supporter of the Bowser and Birdie series.

about the author

Spencer Quinn is the author of the *New York Times* best-selling Chet and Bernie mystery books and *The Right Side*, both for adults. His novels for kids include the #1 *New York Times* bestselling Bowser and Birdie novel, *Woof*, and the follow-up, *Arf*, as well as the Edgar Award–nominated Echo Falls series. Spencer lives with his wife, Diana, and dogs, Audrey and Pearl, on Cape Cod, Massachusetts.

Bark if you want more Bowser!

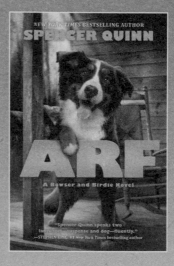

Bowser and Birdie are back with more bad guys, more mysteries, and more bacon.